Never Say
G❤❤dbye....
bonds are forever

Never Say Goodbye....

bonds are forever

Rajiv Seth

Srishti
PUBLISHERS & DISTRIBUTORS

SRISHTI PUBLISHERS & DISTRIBUTORS
N-16, C. R. Park
New Delhi 110 019
srishtipublishers@gmail.com

First published by Srishti Publishers & Distributors in 2012

All characters in this book are fictitious, and any resemblance to real persons, living or dead, is coincidental.

Typeset in AGaramond 12pt. by Suresh Kumar Sharma at Srishti

Prologue

Finally the tears came - and when they came, it was in a torrent that seemed unstoppable. Like a lake in the aftermath of rains, her eyes first filled to the brim and then broke the natural barriers to flood her cheeks and fall to her feet. She tried very hard to control herself, but now she couldn't.

She sat on the bed and sobbed. Her body heaved as if it was detached from her mind and was grieving on its own. She cried now, like a little child who had lost her favourite doll - the one she always wanted beside her, the one to which she would talk endlessly, and the one that meant the world to her. She cried as if she didn't know whether the world could even exist without that doll.

Her husband looked on helplessly. He couldn't really understand the extent of her grief. He couldn't decide whether to reach out to her, or to leave her alone. More importantly, he couldn't decide which CD to put into the latest AIWA music system that he had purchased just two days back. But then he thought may be loud music wouldn't be the right antidote for the moment.

It took a long time for her to compose herself and when she did, she turned to him and asked, "Why did he do it?"

Sunil merely shrugged and said "Beats me - probably some personal problem of his". He turned to the bedside table and picked up the hand held video game lying there. He switched it on and tried to absorb himself in the intricacies of avoiding the on- coming obstacles.

"You know Anjali, the graphics on this game are so realistic that you feel as if you're actually on a racing track. These Japanese really know what people would open up their wallets to. Do you know how much I paid for this little thing?" Sunil still had his head down, deep in concentration on the small screen.

Anjali looked up sharply and hissed, "Turn that damn thing off, will you!"

Outside their room, she could hear the start of another of those commotions which were so common in their household. She could hear Ajay, her brother-in-law, arguing heatedly with the cook as to why the onions in the salad had been cut so thick, whilst Devika, his wife, yelled out to Sunil and her to come and join them for lunch.

"Coming?" asked Sunil, as he put the game on pause.

"You go. I'm not hungry. I think I'll skip lunch today," said Anjali.

Alone in the room now, she gave a half smile to herself as she realised that nothing would change even with Aakash gone. Her big family and the rest of the world would just move on, as if nothing very much had happened. Did it really matter if there was one less star in the beautiful sky of ours? Nobody counts them anyway! But for the person who had looked up so often at that one star which shone brighter than the rest, which was closer than the rest, the sky would appear empty if that star disappeared.

Anjali got up from the bed and drew the curtain aside. It was then that she recollected that even the view from the window had been barred with the new air-conditioners installed in the window. Both brothers had decided to buy big air conditioners which could heat all the rooms. None of them liked the messy coal which was used in the fire places of almost all houses in Shillong. Anjali, on the other hand, loved the fireplace which was there in her room. She could sit for hours watching the flames play with each other, giving her a warmth that would fill her with vibrancy, ready to take on the cold world outside. The day both the brothers had decided to do away with coal and go in for very expensive imported air conditioners, she had protested.

"What a lot of money," she had said. "There's such a lot of poverty around. People don't even have money to buy wood to burn. And then, if we have so much money, why don't we give some to my lab. There's always a crunch of funds there."

"No way," said Sunil. "We're in the twenty first century. Let's be modern".

The huge window which she used to open, to get a view of the pine trees outside, was closed to fit the air conditioner. Anjali recollected how claustrophobic she had felt that day. She felt the same way again today. A tremendous urge to get away from it all seized her. She went out quietly, nobody seeing her slipping out, until slowly the din in the dining hall faded and she was alone. She walked on until she reached the little grove of pine trees behind the house. There was a short stump on which she would sit when she wanted to work quietly on whatever lab work she would bring home. And she would carry some nuts to throw to the squirrels that would creep up to her expectantly.

As soon as she sat on the stump, the squirrels came out hesitatingly. But today she had nothing to offer. She didn't even notice the squirrels initially. And when she did, she saw that the squirrels were moving away, as if they too didn't want to share her melancholy.

In the solitude of the forest, Anjali's mind went back to the events of the last forty eight hours. Just that one telephone call - and then onwards, the world seemed to be moving in slow motion.

"Aakash has killed himself," Sunil announced. "I always told you he was a bit crazy."

For once the household turned silent. Anjali was too stunned to react. All she could hear was her heart pounding as if she was rushing up a big hill. She felt faint - and then realised that she had not been breathing.

Her five year old daughter Tanvi broke the silence "But, Aakash uncle was my favourite uncle. If he is dead, I'll have to find another favourite uncle. I don't want to."

Her son, Karan, came across to her side and held her hand. He was just ten, but at that moment he felt grown up enough to understand.

From amongst the pine trees, Anjali felt she could see him smiling at her. He walked through, with that funny swagger of his and rushed past her. Or had he fleetingly kissed her forehead? She gasped and then realised that it was just the wind.

"Damn you!" she said, half aloud.

Why did he have to be so different from others? How could a guy play with his own death? Wasn't he ever scared?

Anjali remembered that stupid looking old jeep of his. She used to tease him about it, but secretly, she had always been a bit jealous of the lavish affection that Aakash would shower on that little 'Dinky'. That's what he would always call his jeep.

He would so often drive up to Laitkor peak, the highest peak in Shillong, his 'Dinky' filled with little Khasi children from the villages around there. There would be yells and screams as he would tear down the hairpin bends and the little urchins would have had their treat for the day. Aakash loved children.

But the day before yesterday had been different. He had gone up to the peak as usual, but this time he didn't pile up the children in his 'Dinky'. In his broken & disjointed Khasi he made the kids understand that he was going to show them some tricks on his jeep.

He revved up. The children yelled and screamed as usual. The jeep picked up speed and the children watched wide eyed, with their mouths open, as it went over the big hump at the edge of the road. It seemed as if it hung in the air for a while and then pitched down and went over the cliff.

The little urchins watched, fascinated, as it tumbled down the hill. They clapped furiously until they saw bigger people come rushing up to the edge of the cliff. They saw the jeep exploding in a ball of fire as it continued going down. And then they stopped clapping as they realised that something was wrong - something was terribly, terribly wrong.

Sunil had gone to help in pulling out the body. Anjali had decided not to go. For a while she thought that maybe she should have.

But, she wanted to keep her memories of Aakash as she had seen him last.

The funeral was held the next day. It was a very quiet affair. A whole lot of people had turned up, but they walked past silently, just looking at Aakash in awe. A lot of them muttered words of thanks for all that he had done for them. There were very few relatives. Except for his father, Anjali couldn't really make out who was who among the scattering of distant aunts and uncles who had arrived for the ceremony. Leaving Sunil behind, Anjali had walked up to Aakash's father and stood next to him - both of them quiet and lost in their own thoughts.

Her mind wandered to one of the many poems which Aakash had written for her. One of them, she almost recited from memory now.

When I die,
you mustn't cry !
Just raise a finger
and stop that pearl of a tear
rolling down the smoothness of your cheek.
Lift it off and place it on a rose.
Close your eyes
and think of all the good times we had.
- think of when we laughed together.
- think of when we clowned together.
- think of when we dreamt together.
- think of when I held your hand
and tried to show you the way to the stars.

Then seal those thoughts
with a gentle kiss on the rose.
Lay that rose down
beside my face on my pyre.
Let it burn with me
so that the ashes of what I cherished
mingle with my ashes
and dissipate into nothingness.
For that is what
life is all about !

Anjali took a deep breath and controlled her emotions. She had no intention of crying. But she needn't have worried. She had suddenly become like a stone - cold, aloof and very clinical in her view of things happening around her. She was very surprised. Aakash used to laugh so much at her ability to cry at the smallest of things. And here she was, standing before him, with no tears in her eyes. She had bought the biggest red rose that she could find. Then she went up and placed it next to him.

Now, standing next to his father, she watched as the others placed flowers on Aakash's body. For her, the rose stood out as if it was the only one placed there.

After a while, they started putting logs of wood on the pyre. Slowly Aakash's face was hidden. That was the last that she would see of him. Four or five of the '*pundits*' starting reciting some hymns and, as if on cue, some of the uncles and aunts joined in. Anjali tried to catch the words, but couldn't. One of the '*pundits*' dipped a log in some melted clarified butter, lit it and handed it over to Aakash's father. He moved up to the pyre and, very mechanically, went around it three times, before lighting it.

As the flames leapt up, one of Aakash's aunts came in front of Anjali and she had to crane her neck to be able to see the pyre. She felt as if she was being pushed out of Aakash's life. She turned around, looked for Sunil, and then she moved backward through the crowd, to go next to him once again.

A gust of cold wind brought her back to the present. Anjali shivered and pulled her shawl close to her. She looked around at the trees, at the little stumps with no one else sitting on them and at the small open patch with none of the squirrels there anymore. She turned and looked at the house where she lived. It was just about a hundred yards away, but it seemed to be far, far away from her.

Suddenly she was lonely, very lonely. A wave of anger surged through her - anger directed at Aakash for leaving her alone - anger which made her half mumble to herself, speaking to a non-existent Aakash. "Why did you show me another path in life - a superior one to all the others - when you were not going to tread on it with me? Why have you left me like this - feeling totally lonely and helpless now? Why did you do it?"

Tanvi had crept up quietly, to stand next to Anjali. When she looked up, Anjali saw her looking with a curious expression on her face. "Who were you talking to, Mamma?"

Tanvi was still in her school uniform and was obviously excited about something. She didn't even wait for Anjali's answer. She jumped onto her lap and said, "Mamma, school was fun today. Guess what I got from there?"

Anjali hugged her close and thought to herself, "I wonder if Tanvi will ever know what she has lost?"

1

Devika Chauhan grew up like most Indian girls do. She was, as her father put it, protected from the vagaries of the world. She was a girl, and therefore she needed to spend more time at home learning culinary delights, so that when she got married, her husband could revel in that knowledge.

From the time she was ten years old, she remembers being able to make '*chapaties*'- which were the mainstay of the meals in their house. Of course, initially the *chapaties* would be of all shapes except round and her two brothers would laugh their guts out. But it remained an issue in the house till she produced round and fluffed up *chapaties*.

Her father, Mr. Satish Chauhan, had risen from a clerk to become the Station Master of the railway station at Bareilly, a small city about 250 Km. from Delhi. For him, the rise had been phenomenal. He had achieved his life's ambition and it didn't matter to him whether the Congress party remained in power or whether the opposition took over. Whether Rajiv Gandhi continued as the Prime Minister of India or not, was not his concern. Mr. Chauhan had reached the zenith of his career and all that really mattered was that the trains originating from his station left in time every day.

On most days, he would go home a satisfied man. He had two sons. So what if they weren't too devoted to studies. He was sure he would be able to get them jobs in either the railways or in some bank. They had grown up tough and he was certain that they could fend for themselves. Maybe they, too, could rise slowly from being clerks to becoming officers in some organisation!

He sipped his tea and settled down in front of the television set. He thought of getting up to put it on, but then felt too lazy to make the effort. Instead, he looked at the photographs of his sons which were framed and took their pride of place on top of the television set. He looked proudly at them. These two would carry his name to the next generation. Then if even one of them has a son, it would carry on to the generation after that. His heart swelled with pride.

For quite some time now, his wife had been telling him to put Devika's photograph there too. "After all," she had said, "Devika is our first born."

But Mr. Satish Chauhan thought it was a waste. "She's here with us for a few more years. Then we'll get her married. Her place will be in her in-laws' house."

In the meanwhile, Devika grew up. She had gone to school because all other children went to school. The first available school was good enough for her. And it was walking distance from their house. So it was best for everyone. It was a girls' school and it didn't insist on a uniform. So that saved money for better clothes for the boys. Mr. Chauhan wasn't really sure as to what was taught to Devika in the eleven years that she went to that school. It wasn't really important.

Of course, in the case of the boys, an effort was put in to find a good convent school. St Joseph's fitted the bill. The two boys had to grow up to be budding gentlemen.

Like many other children in many other houses, Mr. Chauhan's children also had their fights at home. The reasons for the fights were generally nothing very much. The range varied between who should open the door when the bell rang to who should lay the table for dinner. There was enough scope in the reasons, for victory or defeat. But Devika always lost. In fact she wondered why she fought at all. Whenever victory seemed imminent, one of her brothers would make such a hue and cry that her father would move in faster than the Secretary General of the United Nations and then Devika would, just like one of the countries of the third world, be told to shut up or else.

Devika closed her mind to all the things she didn't like at her house. Slowly, she withdrew from everyone. It was, but natural then, that when she went to college, she became a very different person. She was boisterous, she was outgoing and friendly and she loved the company of her friends. She spent a lot of time with them.

In that period, she developed the fine art of lying. Life was much easier that way. She would skip a lot of her classes and would go to watch movies while she should have been in college. She would glibly lie to her professors and she would equally easily lie to her mother about her whereabouts.

The celluloid world became part of her life. She started living in a dream world, where she was the centre of attraction - where she was important - where her feelings mattered. In any case, the three hours or so in which the reels rolled, transported her to a different life of glamour, glitz and money. She sometimes wished she could just walk into the screen and be part of that story!

Devika was now part of a group of ten girls - all rebels of some sort or the other. In the group, Devika was acknowledged as a leader. She insisted on doing things her way and her charm would move the group with her. They would sit together in class. They would go for movies together. They would want to discuss their homes - but here Devika would almost always get them to change the topic.

She respected her father and she loved her mother and brothers. But she had dreamt of much more. She felt that the five of them led five different lives. None of them even had any common interests. She missed small things like having gone out together for a picnic or having sat together and played cards. She missed the closeness that she saw in other families and this especially, hurt her to a very great extent.

In Bareilly College most romances originate at the college canteen and they get fuelled by numerous cups of coffee in winters and bottles of Thums Up in summers - Cokes and Fantas having been banished from India for quite a few years.

It started with a "Hi beautiful" and a "Hi handsome" routine between Deepak and Devika, but slowly settled down to what might be called a steady romance. More appropriately, it should have been called a steady college-time romance. Devika never spoke about Deepak at home. Nor did they ever plan to meet outside college hours. This kind of an arrangement only led to missed classes and bad results. Deepak was quite smitten by Devika's charm and was very sure in his mind that he wanted the relationship to develop into a lasting one. Devika, on the other hand, wasn't too sure. She seemed to have decided on a course for her life.

Bareilly was still a small town. It hadn't yet woken up to the needs of the younger generation. There were no discotheques as yet. There were very few well maintained parks where a young couple could sit quietly for a few hours and talk to their heart's content. Even the few parks which existed were, in sorts, the permanent home of a whole lot of beggars and urchins who had nowhere else to go.

So Deepak and Devika had very few options. At the college canteen they were invariably in the midst of others. Roaming around in the gardens of the college was one way of being alone with each other. Here they would talk for hours - getting to know each other better and pouring out their worries to each other.

"My mother has been after me to give the IAS exams," said Deepak one day. "I don't want to."

"But you've got to take a decision sooner or later," Devika said. "You've got to make up your mind and do something."

"What about you?"

"I'm pretty sure about my future. I know I won't be allowed to work till I get married. I'll be able to work only after that."

"Then why don't we plan it together. Think of what I should do and later, you can join up in that" suggested Deepak.

"But you live in a joint family. Your mother and your elder *bhabi* - do you think they would agree to my working somewhere?"

"No. No, I'm quite sure they wouldn't. But why think of that right now. We'll work out something after we get married."

Devika just kept quiet, engrossed in thought.

"Hey, come on," said Deepak, "let's go and have lunch in a restaurant."

"But do we have enough money?" asked Devika.

"It's the beginning of the month. Let's blow up my pocket money. We can scrounge for the rest of the month."

"Okay," said Devika.

They went to the restaurant of Chandragupta Hotel and had a Tandoori meal. There was a *'ghazal'* singer on stage, who was doling out some sentimental songs. At the end of it, Deepak felt that it was all worth the agony of having to spend the rest of the month with very little money in his pocket.

The romance lasted only a year. The day she completed her final exams, Mr. Chauhan called Devika for one of the rare chats he had with her.

"You have finished college now!" he started.

"That's quite a profound statement," Devika wanted to say. But she kept quiet, waiting for more. She could almost guess what was coming up.

"We've been looking for a boy who would make an ideal husband for you," said her father. "Your *bua*, who lives in Delhi, has suggested one, who she thinks would be right. We've agreed to the match. They're coming here next week for the engagement ceremony."

"What does he do?" asked Devika.

"They've got a family business in automobile spare parts in Delhi. It's quite a flourishing business and I believe they have a lot of money."

That was the first block in the jigsaw of life which Devika had planned for herself. It seemed to be fitting-in quite well. In the last three years she had realised that money would play a central role in her life. She would need money to be important. She would need money to move places. Above all, she would need money to have confidence in herself.

Her father pulled out an envelope from between the folds of a newspaper lying on the table in front of him.

"This is his photograph. Here, take a look."

Devika took the photograph and casually glanced at it. A handsome young man stared back at her.

"Nice. Quite nice, really," she said.

Actually, however, it didn't matter. This wasn't even a piece in the scheme of things. Her jigsaw could have been completed even if the boy was not good looking.

"And his parents . . . . ?" she left it hanging.

"Oh," said her father. "That's the only problem. Both of them have passed away. The two brothers now live by themselves in a big house in Greater Kailash."

With almost an audible clang, the second piece fitted in. The excitement must have showed on her face because her father looked at her curiously.

"His brother - is he married?" she wanted to know.

"No. This boy, Ajay, is the eldest."

The third and final piece fell into place. Devika was flush with excitement. She couldn't believe her luck. This was exactly what she wanted - to be in a position where others would listen to her.

She never met Deepak again.

When Ajay Sharma and his brother came to see them the next week, Devika put on her best saree. She exuded charm. She talked about automobiles as if she knew a lot about them. Ajay was almost swept off his feet.

On a very pleasant evening in March 1986, Devika and Ajay got married in a glittering function at the Claridges Hotel in New Delhi. Devika Chauhan went into history. Devika Sharma emerged - a new, dynamic personality. It was as if she had opened a door and gone into a new world. In her mind, she closed the door and decided never to look back again.

When all the functions of the wedding were over, Mr. Satish Chauhan had a small celebration at home. He insisted that both his sons be present. One of his major responsibilities was taken care of.

He sat back - and heaved a sigh of relief!

2

The welcome address was given by Dr. Narasimha. The entire hall was silent, with the freshers sitting in awe - awe of the occasion and awe of the man who spoke. It looked as if years of toil and hard work had given him the lines on his face. He looked stern and the type of person who wouldn't even think of mixing any fun with his profession.

"My name is Dr. Narasimha," the man with the same name announced. "I am the Dean of Student Affairs, and it is my job to welcome you all here and to a new world."

Anjali Kothari moved her eyes around the impressive lecture hall of the All India Institute of Medical Sciences, popularly known as AIIMS. She didn't have the guts to move her head, but she couldn't resist looking at people around her.

"You all here," said the Dean, "have taken the first step to becoming doctors. In the next four years, you will go through an extremely rigorous routine. You will have no time for anything but your books. No one has probably collated this information, but it is my guess that each one of you would go through about thirty thousand pages of medical literature before you graduate from this institute."

Anjali felt challenged. With every one of the difficulties that the Dean drew their attention to, she felt more and more determined that she would do well. Somehow, challenges always stimulated her.

"For those of you who think that your hard work will be over after these four years, let me tell you that you are wrong. A doctor remains a student through his or her life. And for those of you, who have come into this profession for the money involved, let me tell you that that's just a corollary and not the theorem. The theorem is that you are joining a noble profession for a noble cause. A few years later, people will depend on you, they would rely on your decisions, a lot of lives would depend on your decisions. And these decisions would be influenced to a very large extent by what you learn at this institute and the work that you put in here," the dean lectured.

For a moment, Anjali's mind drifted to her parents. She would never be able to forget the expressions on their faces when the medical entrance examination results were declared. They hugged her as if she had done it all for them. In a way, she had. Just the joy on their faces had made it all worth it. And now, she looked forward to the day when she would go home with a degree in her hand.

"You still have a chance. If I have scared you, or if you are squeamish about the hard work to be put in, you are at liberty to get up and walk away right now. Because after this, your hands will be locked in the hands of the faculty of this institute and believe me, their grip is pretty tough."

Just like a toddler, who finds the first step very difficult, so is it in the life of a medical student.

Human Anatomy classes were what the faint hearted dreaded the most. The first sight of a human cadaver made a lot of them hold their breaths. Putting the blade to make the first incision brought bile to many mouths.

"Take your time," encouraged Dr. Joshi, their professor of Physiology. "Be sure of where you want to reach before you make the incision. Don't be in a hurry, your cadavers won't go away."

"How insensitive can he be?" said Menaka, standing next to Anjali.

"I guess we all have to become like that," answered Anjali.

"This man, whose body we are going to dissect in the next few days, died a week back at this institute," Dr Joshi announced.

There was a suppressed groan all around.

Dr Joshi waited a while before continuing. "I know, death is a very difficult thing to face. So let us be grateful to this man and his family for letting us use this body for the sake of science. Don't waste this sacrifice. Learn all that you can in as short a while as possible."

They learnt, slowly and steadily, from the professors and from each other. They would be quizzed, even in anatomy practicals. Anjali usually did well.

Dr Joshi moved aside layers of muscle one day, pointed to the lower end of the stomach and asked "What is this?"

"This is the pyloric sphincter. It controls the emptying of chyme - that's food changed into a semi fluid by the stomach - into the small intestine. This sphincter is a thickened band of circular muscles. Waves of peristalsis push the chyme through the opening formed by this sphincter into the small intestines," Anjali replied.

"Hmm," was all that Dr Joshi would say. But generally, a 'Hmm' could be interpreted as a compliment.

Anjali shared a room with a Bengali girl called Sumitra. She was from Basirhat, a small town near Kolkatta. Sumitra was a cheerful girl. In fact, one could call her a compulsive talker. There was never a dull moment with her. It was as if she always had something to tell.

There was only one thing which would worry her. That was her knack of reading the wrong thing for an exam. It was not that she wouldn't study hard. It was just that there was a tremendous contrast between the two roommates. Anjali would study a tenth of what Sumitra did, and then she would roam around the institute, lending a helping hand here and there. Sumitra, on the other hand, constantly pored over her books.

The late night routine had almost become a ritual.

"Sumitra, please put off the light," Anjali would plead from her bed. "Just a few minutes more," Sumitra would say. "And, hey Anju, since you're awake, quickly explain to me how sound impulses go to the brain."

Anjali opened her eyes and rattled off, "The inner ear contains the Cochlea, a snail shaped spiral tunnel in which the organ of Corti - the true organ of hearing - is located. The organ of Corti consists of specialised nerve cells that follow the spiral of the Cochlea. The cells rest on the basilar membrane, which is made up of connective tissue fibers. The nerve cells have hair-like projections and the tips of the hairs are in contact with a membrane called the tectorial membrane. The spongy bone that forms the core of the cochlea has many tiny tunnels through which the nerves carry impulses to the brain. Now will you stop eating my brain and go to sleep. I'll explain the rest in the morning."

"Anju, how the hell do you remember all this?"

"That's easy - just concentrate when you study"

Sumitra would sigh - but would continue reading till late at night.

Anjali would remember 30th October 1984 for the rest of her life. She was in a dermatology class when someone came in and whispered something to the professor. He rushed out, his face quite ashen in colour. It was a while later, when another student came in and told them that Indira Gandhi had been shot.

"They've brought her here. She's in the OT, but I heard that there are so many bullets pumped into her, that the chance of her surviving is remote," said the boy excitedly.

By the time they left the classroom, the entire AIIMS seemed to be swarming with people. Very few knew what was happening. Everyone just moved around trying to get bits of information. There were scores of policemen all around. They too, seemed to be waiting for news.

It was a couple of hours before it was known that the Prime Minister was no more. Both Anjali and Sumitra went quietly to their rooms. It was lucky that they did. Because otherwise they would have witnessed the start of some of the most horrifying days that India went through. Days which affected the nation for many years to come and which left scars which would take ages to heal. Agitated mobs killed hundreds of Sikhs. Their houses were burnt and their shops were looted.

It was days before calm returned. The whole of Delhi seemed to be affected. And it had its effect at the Institute, too. Classes were cancelled for two days. A student in the final year, Manjit Basra, lost his father and his brother in the riots. He had left the institute and no one was sure whether he would return or not.

Those few days left a mark on Anjali's psyche. It was as if her faith in human beings had been shaken.

"How can people do this to each other?" she asked her father one day.

"I really don't know. Some very sane people behave very differently when they are in mobs," said her father.

"But don't they have any control over their sense of reasoning? How can human beings behave like animals?"

Her father only shook his head, as if he, himself, was ashamed of the events.

"Papa, do you know what they did to Manjit's father and brother? I think it was just downright disgusting," Anjali continued angrily. "Don't the same people have brothers and fathers? Didn't they for a minute think about how it would have been if their own relatives were involved?"

Her mother brought in dinner. Even the aroma of the fish curry and rice that she had made didn't make any of them feel better and they ate in silence after that.

The years flew by very rapidly. In the initial years, each doctor-to-be dreams about what he or she would go through in later years. Some fixed notions creep in, based on their experiences with doctors in their childhood and their fascination of the subject. Anjali was no exception.

She had the notion that she would determine beautiful one-to-one relationships with her patients when, ultimately, she became a doctor.

"I want my patients to be just mine," she had told Sumitra one day.

"Anju, you're being possessive about them before even one of them has come to you," said Sumitra.

That day they had both laughed about it. But as they neared the completion of the course at AIIMS, they realised that the setting in which medicine was practiced, was undergoing a change. They had almost seen this change as they progressed to the final year. In many cases, they found that the management of the individual patient required the active participation of a variety of trained professional personnel - not only physicians, but also dieticians, biochemists, psychologists and other paramedical personnel.

So they went though the techniques, skills and objectives of colleagues in the fields allied to medicine. They had some guest lectures on biochemistry and here, Anjali would listen, totally enthralled by the world of genetics.

"Sometime in life, I'm going to study genetics," Anjali whispered to the boy sitting next to her."

"Huh, you mean you understand what's going on?"

"Of course I do, and it's so fascinating," Anjali shot back.

After the degree course was over, they underwent a one year internship. Anjali, expectedly, finished with distinctions in almost every subject.

"Are you real?" was the reaction of most of her course mates when they saw her marks.

Her parents were thrilled. Her father had tears in his eyes as he hugged her. But Anjali, now twenty one, felt as if she had moved only one step ahead. She wanted to do much, much more.

"I want to study more, Papa. There's so much more to know. There's so much more to experience."

"Come here and sit. Let's just talk today," said her father. "Tell me what you want to do."

"I want to do research in medicine. I want to study lots and lots more. I want to go into fields which others have been scared to venture into. I don't just want to live for myself I want to do things for others and I want a name for myself."

Her father gave her a kiss on her forehead. "So where do we start?"

"Well first of all I want five hundred rupees to go and buy a new dress for myself. Then I want another five hundred rupees to take you both out to dinner right now. And then I want fifteen thousand rupees to buy a scooter and then..."

They all laughed as they got ready and then they went out to have dinner at Karnataka Sangha at Moti Bagh. None of them liked going to fancy restaurants. They loved this small little place which could hardly boast about its decor, but it had few competitors in the quality of its dishes. Anjali's father loved the dosas there. So they all had dosas.

After all, today was his day.

Anjali had a flood of job offers once her internship finished. It wasn't just her marks which helped. In that one year, she worked so hard that she made a name for herself. Doctors she worked with talked to each other about interns. With most interns, the end of the degree phase gave them a feeling of freedom and they did tend to look at the period of internship as a hurdle before they got on to a job. Some, amongst them, felt like doctors already and this hampered their learning process.

This was not so with Anjali. In fact, to her, the period of internship was the busiest time she had. Her insatiable appetite for learning was whetted even more as she now experienced various diseases and injuries as she moved from department to department.

Her reputation preceded her, when she took up a job as a resident doctor at Safdarjung Hospital, a government run hospital very close to AIIMS. She had discussed it with her father, before taking up the job.

"Why this hospital?" asked her father.

"Everyone's asking me the same question," said Anjali. "They seem to think that I should have gone in for the hospital which would pay me the most."

"So why didn't you?" her father asked, even though he already knew what her answer would be.

"Well I've seen some of the private hospitals. What hit me first was that if you were ill with some odd disease, you wouldn't have been able to afford to go there. I saw a family, once, pleading at the reception to admit a young boy. He was delirious with high fever. But the staff insisted that they first needed the advance. The boy's mother kept saying that they would arrange the money in a few days. But no, they had to go and look for another hospital. Is it fair?"

Mr. Kothari would always get a surge of admiration and affection whenever his daughter got agitated on such topics. And somehow, he always enjoyed goading her on.

"How does all that matter to you, Anjali? You would have got a much better pay packet," he said.

"But would I be happier?" asked Anjali.

"*Beta*, knowing you, you'd be happy only when others appreciate your hard work," said her father.

"Papa, you have told me so much about *Karma*. You have taught me that doing things for others is the biggest pay packet that a human being can get. That's why I've chosen this hospital, where there will be a variety of patients - lots of whom won't be able to afford a private hospital."

For a young doctor, it was surprising how fast Dr. Anjali Kothari acquired a reputation for herself. What she enjoyed the most, was the Medical OPD, because it was here that she would meet her patients for the first time, listen carefully to their symptoms and then give her diagnosis.

Anjali looked for a guide and mentor in the hospital – and found one in Dr. Sunayana Ghosh, a doctor five years her senior and a medical specialist at Safdarjung Hospital ever since she finished her MD. Very quickly, they built up a rapport between themselves. Dr. Sunayana had an infectious laugh and serious as she was, Anjali found a lot of satisfaction in the contrast between them. Off duty, Anjali would drop in at Sunayana's home quite often. They would invariably end up talking about medicine all the time since Sunayana's husband was also a doctor. He was an orthopaedic surgeon with a private practice which was picking up quite rapidly.

"Couldn't you find something better to do in life?" asked Anjali, "– than picking on other people's bones?"

"And what do you two ladies have to do? Collect a couple of symptoms from a patient and give a diagnosis. If it works – it's your good luck. If it doesn't, it's the poor guy's bad luck!"

"Oh, it's far better than using those funny looking tools that you have in your OT. They're literally saws and drills and – Oh God, they remind me of the tools that Sher Singh, our carpenter carries with him!" Sunayana argued.

"It's a job of skill, ma'am – a job where we use our hands to put things together. Not like your field. Nowadays if a guy has fever, you give him a wide-spectrum antibiotic. And if he has something more serious, you still give him the same. Heck, I could do that sitting at home."

"Oh, shut up, you know it's not like that," said Sunayana.

Invariably Anjali would be the one to butt in and end the silly arguments in that house.

"Sunayana, our patients could wait a while for us, but in accidents, an orthopaedic surgeon is the guy in demand," said Anjali.

"Ya," said Sunayana quite grudgingly to her husband, "if I were to break my leg, I'd have to come to you!"

"At least then you couldn't walk out on me!"

Anjali just loved their company – and that of their two year old son. Sometimes she would wish to herself that when she settled down, she too could have a husband who was a doctor. Life could be so much fun that way.

Two years went by.

"Paging for Dr. Anjali - - Paging for Dr. Anjali - - Please report to Ward 6." The familiar call over the tenoy system had now become a part of her life.

Life settled down to a routine. She bought a second hand Maruti car, with her father financing a part of it. That made her more independent. She didn't have to worry now about late nights or coming across to see a patient at an odd hour.

Anjali was twenty four and, predictably, her mother would bring up the topic of marriage every now and then. Predictably too, her father would veto the topic.

"Anjali is a mature girl. She wants to study more – she wants to do research. Let her settle down in her career first."

"Yes Papa," she hugged him, "Mr. Anjali can wait – can't he?"

"Poor guy," said Mr. Kothari, as he went back to his newspaper.

Anjali spent a lot of time at the hospital. A major portion of the rest was spent poring over books, keeping herself abreast with the latest medicines and the research on newer ones.

Until the tennis match at Ramjas college …!

3

"Anjali, we're both taking the afternoon off today," Sunayana announced as she stormed into the room.

"Why, what's happened?"

"A cousin of mine is playing a tennis match. It's the finals of some tournament and he kept insisting that I come. My car is with my husband. So lucky you, you've been nominated as chauffeur to Dr. Sunayana Ghosh. Let's go."

"Tennis? But I don't know head or tail about it."

"It doesn't matter. You don't have to toss."

"No really, I don't even know how it's played."

"Great – you don't have to play even one set!"

"Sunayana, my patients…?" was one last plea from Anjali.

"Anjali, learn to have some time for yourself."

Anjali took her car. It was a long drive from the hospital to Ramjas College. On the way, Sunayana took it on herself to acquaint Anjali with the game.

"Oh, you'll enjoy it. There'll be two guys with racquets who'll seem to be taking out their anger on one little yellow ball. All they have to do is literally – put the ball in the other guy's court. And the guy who puts it more often in the other guy's court wins."

"I know that much. I've seen my Dad watching tennis sometimes," said Anjali.

"Okay, then let me switch to scoring. That's the best part of tennis. There'll be a lot of romance in the air. Every game starts with the umpire calling 'Love all'. And then, while you're still wondering about the enormity of the task, a couple of balls here and there and he calls a slightly saner 'Love fifteen'!"

The traffic was thin in the afternoon and they reached the courts at the college earlier than they anticipated.

"There he is," said Sunayana, pointing at a player at the nets.

She waved out to him. He stopped playing and came across to where they were standing.

"Sunayana, it's so nice to see you. Thanks for coming."

"Sunil, meet Anjali. She's also a doctor, working with me at the hospital." Sunayana did the introductions.

"Hi." Sunil held out his hand to Anjali. "I didn't know we were going to have glamorous guests at this match."

Anjali blushed at once. She tried to say something but all she managed were a few incoherent sounds.

"Who's playing against you?" asked Sunayana.

"Okay. Let me get you up to date. We've been playing an inter-collegiate tournament and I'm representing Ramjas College. I really don't know how, but I've made it to the finals. That's what you're going to watch now. I'm playing against Rishi Ranjan of Khalsa College, and he's superb. So you've probably come all the way just to watch him make mincemeat of me."

"Oh come on, I've heard that you're pretty good too," said Sunayana.

"No, seriously, this chap – Rishi – he's almost a pro. If I manage to win a few games, I'll be quite happy."

While Sunayana and Sunil were chatting, Anjali found herself looking at Sunil. Something about him charmed her. She looked at his powerful biceps and his broad shoulders. She looked at the boyish look on his face.

"Was she lusting for a man?" she thought.

Quite embarrassed, she turned away and looked around at the crowds building up in the stands.

Sunil seemed to have prophesised correctly. His opponent broke his serve in the very first game. By the time they completed the fifth game, Sunil was trailing 1-4. A large majority of the crowd consisted of Ramjas students, and they all fell silent as the one sided match continued. Sunil lost the set 1-6.

When Khalsa College won the first game of the second set, everyone was sure that the match would be over in straight sets.

Sunil tossed the ball up for his first serve in the second game and then lobbed it straight into the net. The umpire called 'fault'. In the deathly silence before the second serve, Anjali suddenly cupped her hands to her mouth and yelled "Come on Sunil, you can do it."

Sunil paused. He had a half smile on his face as he cocked his head to one side, as if to acknowledge her goading. When he served, it was an ace. He went on to keep his serve at 40-0.

In the third game, when Sunil broke service, the Ramjas guys were all on their feet and when he went on to win the set 6-4, they broke into cheers.

With the excitement mounting, the third set was a cliffhanger.

Sunayana was quite amused at Anjali's involvement in the game. "I thought you didn't know anything about tennis?"

"You taught me on the way, didn't you?"

The game was level at 6 games each and then went into the tie breaker. Sunil won 7-6.

As he threw his racquet up in the air, his friends rushed over to him, almost lifting him off the court. When he managed to extricate himself, he came across to Sunayana and Anjali.

"Thanks for cheering me up, Anjali. That really helped," he said as he toweled himself.

"Oh, you played well. I think you just needed a bit of confidence in yourself. Your backhand volleys left your opponent helpless," said Anjali.

"Backhand volleys? Hold it, hold it…," said Sunayana. "I thought you didn't know anything about tennis?"

"I learn fast, don't I?"

They all laughed.

As Sunayana and Anjali turned to leave, Sunil held out his hand to Anjali. Her hand felt small and comfortable in his. The handshake was, noticeably, a bit longer than it should have been.

That wee bit longer was all that it took for Anjali to decide that this was the man she was going to marry.

She waited for a call from him. At times, she thought that she should call him. But she didn't have his number. She didn't even know where he stayed. And she definitely didn't want to go up to Sunayana and ask her. Anyway, she thought, if he's interested, he'll call.

At the end of two weeks she gave up the wait. Maybe he already had a girlfriend. Maybe she wasn't his type. Maybe ——.

So when he did call, she wasn't expecting it.

"Hi Anjali, remember me...?"

Anjali hesitated. "No..., who is this?"

"I'm probably the only guy whose backhand you've appreciated!"

"Sunil...?" Anjali tried hard to conceal her excitement.

"I thought I'd call much earlier, but my brother had sent me to Bombay for some business deals. I got back just yesterday."

"You missed so much of college?"

"Oh, it keeps happening. The family business is more important."

"More important than studies?"

"God – stop nagging me. Uh, Anjali, how about coming with me for a cup of coffee one of these days?" There was a bit of hesitation in Sunil's voice.

"Sure. I think I'd like that. When?" asked Anjali.

"How about tomorrow?"

"No. I'm on duty tomorrow. Shall we make it the day after?"

"Lovely. I'll pick you up at five and then I'll drop you home."

They had what others called a whirlwind romance. For the first time since she took up medicine, Anjali started looking forward to free time so that she could go out somewhere with Sunil. She was, of course, too much of a professional to neglect her work even at the height of her romance. Sunil would keep grumbling about it, but after a while he got used to it.

At restaurants and coffee houses, they would chat for hours whenever they got a chance. Right from the beginning, Sunil insisted on going to classy places. Anjali never ever got impressed, but then all she wanted was to be in his company and any place was good enough.

It wasn't too long before Anjali was convinced that she had found the man of her dreams.

For Sunil it was just a dream come true. The opinion of others mattered a great deal for him in any matter. How he was appreciated by others was very important to him. And so was it when it came to Anjali. The fact that she was beautiful and that she was acknowledged by others as being so, made him feel on top of the world. On top of that, she was a doctor. Sunil could never believe his luck.

He brought up the topic of marriage just about a month later.

"When shall we get married?" asked Sunil one day.

Although she knew it was coming, Anjali wasn't too sure how to react.

"I'll talk to my father," she said.

When she did, she wasn't prepared for her parents' reactions either.

"How can you marry a boy who's a whole year younger to you?" wailed her mother.

"Mama, how is that an issue? It's more important that the boy I marry is the right one for me. I know him so well now. He's such a gentle and caring chap."

"And a chap who's had to repeat two years in college," her father butted in.

"But I told you that he couldn't do well because he had to spend so much time in his business."

"What business do they do, if it's any business of mine?" asked her father.

"They sell automobile parts."

Mr. Kothari merely grimaced.

The grimace was still there when Anjali brought Sunil to meet them. Mr. Kothari seemed to have made up his mind that he was not going to like Sunil. The conversation was strained and both Sunil and Anjali were relieved when the ordeal was over.

"I don't think he likes me," said Sunil when they met the next day.

"Are you marrying him – or me?" asked Anjali, and that shut him up.

The visit to Sunil's house was quite a contrast. Sunil had already had a long talk with his brother and Devika.

Ajay, being elder, took it on himself to be sure that the match would be alright.

"A doctor in our house? Will she be able to adjust?" he asked.

"I'm sure she will," Sunil replied.

"But will she be able to look after the house like your *Bhabi* does? Ajay persisited.

As would always be the case, Sunil turned to Devika, and then when Devika took over the thought process in the house, Ajay's views faded into the background.

"She's elder to you? Well,... I don't know. I hope she'll be able to look after you," Devika said.

"*Bhabi*, it's very important for me to have a wife who is good looking and who my friends will look up to. That'll raise my value in their eyes. It really is important to me."

"I know that, Sunil. I know that pretty well now," said Devika. "Call her across anytime you want. Let's all meet her and welcome her into this family."

"*Bhabi*, I love you," Sunil almost yelled as he hugged her.

As usual there had been a lot of deliberation in Devika's mind before she had decided. Anjali was a doctor and that was important to her and her family. They were in a business and, although they were well off, they needed to reinvest most of the profits to make the business grow. If there was one person with a fixed salary who they could bank on, then it was like a fixed deposit. Of course, it was very foolish of her to work in a government hospital but then Devika was sure she would be able to work on her and get her to shift to a big private hospital where she would earn much more.

Anjali was welcomed when she came to the Sharma household. She was particularly attracted to Devika who she thought was charming.

"She's my mother and father all combined into one," said Sunil when he introduced Devika to Anjali.

The meal laid out was a simple one, but it was laid out in a manner which made Anjali feel very important. Devika and Ajay kept talking to her as if they knew her for long.

All at once Anjali felt that she and Devika would get along very well.

At that time she didn't realise how wrong she was.

4

In India it is always the boy's side which dictates terms at any wedding. And so, although Mr. Kothari would have preferred a simple and quiet wedding for his daughter, it turned out to be a big affair. Devika had insisted that there would be some politicians and some wealthy businessmen as guests. The guest list itself slowly increased from a small number to over five hundred. Reluctantly, Mr. Kothari changed the venue of the marriage from the lawns on the side of their house to Claridges Hotel.

"I got married there, Uncle, and the hotel had done a wonderful job," said Devika.

Just a week earlier Mr. Kothari had gone to Chandni Chowk to locate the *halwai* who had done all the cooking at his own wedding almost thirty years ago. That *halwai* had died, but his son was in the same profession and everything was tied up quickly.

Now, as he walked into Claridges Hotel, he was conscious of the fact that he was feeling very out of place. But one look at the excitement on Anjali's face was enough to vitalize him.

In spite of giving-in to what he described as a commercialisation of the ceremony, Mr. Kothari insisted on arranging a few items required for the ceremony, which he felt would uphold the traditionality of an Indian wedding. Fresh flowers – to signify the beauty of nature, Coconuts – to signify fertility, since a coconut is a complete fruit that contains both food and water, Rice & Jaggery – representing grain foods which are necessary for the subsistence of human life, *Ghee* – to feed the sacred fire and *Kumkum* – to mark the forehead for good luck.

The actual ceremony began with a *Ganesh Puja*- a worship of Lord Ganesh and went on to the *Pani Grahana* and *Pratigya* – taking of vows. Then there were the *Mangal Pheras* – where a small, open fire was lit in the centre of the *Mandap* so that the fire may act as a witness to the marriage. Fire is regarded as a source of energy by Hindus and it is believed that only fire has the capacity to separate the bond of unity between the bride and the groom.

When the ceremony was nearing the end, and as all the relatives and friends sprinkled rice and blossoms over the newly married couple and offered them their *Ashirwad* - or blessings, Mr. Kothari had tears in his eyes. Anjali noticed, and as they looked at each other she seemed to be telling him that she was still going to be his daughter first of all so what was he crying about. Mr. Kothari looked back ruefully as if to say that he wasn't crying at all. It was just that there were tears in his eyes and he just had no clue as to what to do about them.

At the end of the two weeks leave that she had taken, Anjali found that she was keen to get back to the hospital. Her mind was on her patients.

"There are lots of other doctors there, Anjali," Sunil had tried to argue.

"Yes, but I have a duty to fulfill," said Anjali.

The first day itself was like a whirlpool, which sucked Anjali back to the reality of the hospital. All at once she had a case of head injury, one case of ruptured spleen, two cases of unexplained, persisting high fever and one case of severe jaundice in a young boy.

She stood at the edge of the bed on which eight year old Rahul Khanna was lying, studying his case-sheet and she didn't like what she was reading. He had been admitted to the hospital just three days back with a bilirubin level of 7.0. His blood tests indicated an SGOT, SPOT and SGPT OF 300. His skin had turned yellow in the last two days and he was hardly eating anything. He seemed to be much worse than what the laboratory tests indicated.

"I'm your new doctor, Rahul," said Anjali as she extended her hand towards him.

"Hi…," was all that she managed to get out of him. It sounded so weak that it had her worried.

"I want a repeat of all the blood tests done on him immediately," said Anjali to the nurse doing the rounds with her. "And complete bed rest. No playing around at all."

"You better go home, Anjali," said Sunayana at around 9:30 in the night. "You look tired."

"Ya, I think I've had an overdose today."

"Overdose? Overdose of what?"

"Of patients," said Anjali as she packed her things.

She reached home at around 10 pm. Everyone had had dinner and were in their rooms watching the television. Anjali found it odd because she was used to her mother and father waiting for her whatever time she would get back home. And then there would be a dissection of the day's activities with each one wanting to know what the other had done through the day before they would sit down for dinner.

Anjali called out to Bahadur, their Nepali man servant and asked him to lay out her dinner. She took it into her room and sat with Sunil as he watched a replay of a tennis match between Michael Stich and Boris Becker.

"Hi, how was your day?" asked Sunil.

"Oh just about okay. Except that I had a whole lot of accident cases. And then I'm especially worried about a boy called Rahul."

"What's happened to him?"

"He's got Hepatitis."

"What's that?"

"Jaundice," explained Anjali.

"That's all? What's so serious about that?" asked Sunil.

"His bilirubin level seems to ..."

"Oh great, that's deuce. Now I'm sure Becker will win." Sunil sat up at once, his eyes glued to the television set.

The door of their room was flung open and Devika walked in.

"Hi, Anjali. When did you get back?" asked Devika.

"Just a little while back, *Bhabi*."

"How come you got so late?"

"There were a whole lot of patients and their flow never seemed to stop at all."

"Yes, but I'm sure there must be other doctors too. You're married now and you have to think about the house also."

"I know," said Anjali.

She got up and went to the kitchen to put back her plate. Suddenly she had lost her appetite.

Two days later, Rahul's condition worsened drastically. His bilirubin level reached 16. More importantly his SGOT, SPOT readings inched towards 2000. Glucose was being administered intravenously to avoid the onset of Hypoglycemia.

"How are his stools?" Anjali asked Rahul's mother who had been at his bedside for the last six days.

"They're very black in colour."

That meant that Rahul was bleeding internally. He was intermittently slipping into a coma.

"Will he be alright, doctor?" asked his mother.

Anjali held her hand and squeezed it.

"Have faith in God," she said.

"I have faith in you, doctor."

When Rahul died the next day, his mother sat next to his body and sobbed quite inconsolably.

Anjali went into her room and sat there quietly, staring out of the window for a long time, until Sunayana came looking for her.

"Put on the light at least," said Sunayana. "How can you involve yourself so much in a patient? There are so many others waiting for your attention. Are you going to neglect them, because of just one patient?"

"Why are you talking of him as 'just one patient'?" asked Anjali. "He was the son of that woman out there, who's probably still sitting, absolutely shattered. He was alive just an hour back - maybe thinking of his friends - maybe thinking of ice-cream. His mother was holding his hand so lovingly - maybe thinking of what he would become when he grows up - maybe a doctor. And now suddenly he's just a corpse who'll be tagged and put in the mortuary until his family decides on the last rites."

"I know. But this kind of thing happens every day in every hospital. Are you going to be affected so much by every case in the hospital?"

"It's not fair. He was so young! " Anjali was almost talking to herself.

"I guess it's not fair to anyone who hasn't lived life to its full. So why bring age into it?" said Sunayana.

Sunayana went up close to Anjali and sat next to her. She put her arm around her shoulder. Anjali let out a sigh.

"Do you know what his mother told me just yesterday? She said that she had more faith in me than she had in God. And just see how I've let her down," said Anjali.

"Anjali, all of us doctors go through this phase where we think we can substitute for God. We save a couple of lives and we start thinking that we are more important. But then with most of us it's only a phase in the beginning of our careers. All of us go through a couple of rude shocks before we realise that we have a very small role to play in this whole game of life. So let's just play it sincerely and move on to the next Scene in the next Act."

Anjali remained quiet for a very long time.

Finally she said, "Sunayana, you go ahead. I'll go home in a while."

"No way," said Sunayana. "I'm leaving this place only after you gather your things and go out from here."

When Anjali finally got back to her house, it was past eleven. Everyone had gone to sleep. Bahadur came in quickly from his room to give her a glass of water.

"Shall I lay out your dinner *memsahib*?" he asked.

"No, Bahadur. I've had dinner at the hospital," she lied. "Just give me a glass of milk."

She tiptoed into the room so as not to disturb Sunil. She stripped off her clothes and went to have a shower. As the needles of cool water hit her, she realised how exhausted she was. But she wasn't sleepy. All she wanted was to be able to sit with someone and talk about the happenings of the day.

As she lay down on the bed, Sunil reached out and pulled her towards him.

"Hi, I've been waiting for you for so long," he said.

"You're awake? Great, I wanted to chat with you about the hospital."

"What's new? Has something changed?"

"No, nothing. It's about that child I told you of, two days back."

"Which child?" asked Sunil.

"The one with Hepatitis, remember?"

"What's Hepatitis?"

"Sunil, for God's sake - I told you about a child who had severe jaundice. He died this evening."

"Oh, that's sad."

There was an awkward silence between them for a while, before Sunil leaned across once again and put his arms around Anjali.

"We'll talk about it in the morning," said Sunil as he pulled her towards him once again. "Come to me now."

"No, Sunil, not tonight. I'm tired. I'm very exhausted," said Anjali.

"Don't tell me you are going to be like this every time you come back from the hospital. Why don't you just leave the job then?"

"Please Sunil, try and understand me," Anjali pleaded.

But Sunil had turned over and his back was now facing her.

5

Kashmere Gate lies on one side of Delhi. The actual monument has lost its significance over the years. But the area known as Kashmere Gate always bustles with activity. It is the heart of the business of automobile spare parts in the city.

Had it not been for Sunil, Sharma Motor Parts would have been a very nondescript shop in one of the lanes of this busy market. Ever since Sunil started taking interest in the business, the first thing he insisted on was to make it look as swanky as he could.

"I have designed the exteriors of the shop," he proudly told Anjali when she went there for her first visit.

"That's true," said Devika. "Ajay and I would probably have carried on with the shop in the same state in which it was left to us by Papaji. But Sunil insisted on doing it up and it helped to increase sales. It became evident from the day we reopened after the renovation."

Ajay, standing behind Devika, nodded his head in agreement.

It didn't take long for Anjali to realise that it was not just at home, but also in the business, that Devika called the shots. Ajay always seemed to take the back seat.

"You keep talking about the radiators which you manufacture," Anjali asked Sunil. "Where is that done?"

"Come, I'll show you," said Sunil.

He led her through the lanes to a small opening which was actually a piece of land just behind the shop. Here everything was in contrast with the stylishness of the shop. Workers sat around in a very disorganised manner. One end of the mini factory had the copper tubing area where four young boys used a small machine to bend them into the required size. At another end a very young boy, not more than twelve years old was soldering the various parts together.

Anjali was quite appalled. "Why haven't you done up this place? " she asked.

"That would be a waste of money," replied Sunil. "Who's going to come here to see how things are made."

"But wouldn't you be proud if you had a good factory instead of a dingy one like this?" asked Anjali.

"Oh come on Anjali, learn to be practical. You are too inexperienced in life to realise this, but slowly you'll learn that looking good on the outside is more important than what is inside. Look at me. I buy the most expensive shirts. I must have the logo of Charagh Din on all my shirts. I spend so much time in choosing them. And how about my vests? God, I don't even remember which brand I buy. Nobody ever asks to see the label on them. It's just the same here."

"I don't think I'm convinced," said Anjali. Your logic isn't very appropriate. And then, how about quality control. I thought that would be an important criterion, How do you ensure that, in this kind of a setup?"

"The same argument Anjali, the same argument. People just look at how the exteriors are. Then they pay and they go away."

"But that's not correct, "Anjali protested. "By seeing your shop the customers would be relying on you. You would be letting them down every time they buy something from you."

"Tough luck," Sunil shrugged. "When the parts fail they can come back and buy more of them from us. In the end we have a better turnover too."

They even discussed the issue of child labour.

"Isn't it banned by law? How come we haven't stopped using young kids for work?" Anjali asked.

"Lots of things are banned, Anjali, but if they aren't being enforced, why bother? Everyone is using child labour – it's so cheap!" answered Sunil.

That day Anjali went back home a very disillusioned person. She had expected a different set of values from her husband. She had always thought of him as a very righteous person and when she found that he wasn't, she didn't know how to react.

She went to the hospital the next day and got engrossed in her work. But when she came back home, she went straight to Devika's room.

Quite relieved to find her all alone, she brought up the topic straight away.

"*Bhabi*, I wanted to talk to you about the child labour employed in the factory."

"That's nice," said Devika as she sat up. "I never thought you would get around to taking some interest in the business."

"No, it's not that. It's just that I think it's wrong employing children for such jobs. We can easily get skilled labour for the jobs. They would do a much better job too," said Anjali.

"Yes, but think of how much more we would have to pay them. Wouldn't that cut into our profits? And then we would have to deal with labour problems and unions and what not."

"Okay, but it's wrong using young children for this work," said Anjali. "Especially in today's world where there is so much awareness on the need to send children to school and educating them, instead of making them work."

"Anjali, these are all theories put forward by people who only like to preach. Ask them to run a business and I can bet that they too would do exactly the same." Devika argued.

"But businesses won't grow if we don't think ahead. They would just stagnate. And think of the nation as a whole. We have to think of the future of these children."

"Are you now going to teach us how to run a business?" asked Devika, quite visibly irritated.

As Anjali carried on she could slowly sense that she was not getting anywhere with her arguments. She left it at that.

It was a couple of months later that Devika came home quite excited. She charged into Anjali's room. Sunil had just about got back from work and they were sitting and having tea.

"Guess what," she announced. "I had been after Dr. Yogi for quite some time now to get a good job for you. He's recently opened a multispecialty hospital at Vasant Vihar. He's offered you a job there. They're going to pay you quite a pile. At a guess it would be about three times what you're getting right now."

"Wow!" said Sunil.

For Anjali it was too sudden for her to react at all.

"You can join on the first of next month. But you have to go and meet Dr Yogi next week itself," said Devika.

After Devika left, Anjali quietly listened to Sunil and his thrill at the prospects of her new job.

"These places are very posh," he said. "Very soon they'll give you lots of perks and then we can really move up in life."

"Sunil, the 'place' you're referring to is a hospital," said Anjali very quietly.

"Huh?" asked Sunil, not understanding her.

Anjali went to meet her father the next evening while returning from Safdarjung Hospital.

"What's on my little girl's mind?" he asked when he saw her.

"Don't tell me I've become so transparent that you can make out that I want to discuss something with you," said Anjali.

Anjali told him about the new job and her apprehensions.

"I don't know if I'll be happy with the work there, Papa," said Anjali.

"Then why do you want to shift?"

"Because of the money."

"Has money now become important to you?" asked her father.

"No, but it is important to Sunil and his family," said Anjali.

"Then it is a decision that you have to take yourself," her father told her. "Sometimes your decisions have to be based on what others want and not just on what you want."

"So you think I should go ahead and join the new hospital?"

"No, I didn't say that. All I said was that you have to take the decision yourself."

"Papa, how come you always leave the decisions to me. Can't you ever decide something for me," said Anjali.

"That wouldn't be correct, *beta*. You are grown up enough now."

"And even then I keep coming to you with my problems. I feel nice just talking to you about them!"

'*Chikitsa*' in Hindi means therapy, or therapeutic intervention. That was the name of the new hospital in which Anjali took up her assignment.

Dr. Yogeshwar Dayal was the head of the hospital. He was a very impressive man in his early fifties. A beard tinged with silver enhanced his personality. The years that he had spent in California showed up in the accent that he had picked up.

"Call me Yogi," was how he introduced himself to Anjali. "I'm sure it'll be great to have you around, little lady. Out here you're going to be working along with some great names in medicine and I'm sure you're going to live up to it."

'Yogi' was the name he had picked up for himself back in California and he insisted on it being used in India, too. And 'Little Lady ' was the name he picked up for Anjali and he stuck with it for the rest of her association with *Chikitsa* hospital.

The next one year just passed like a whirlwind, as far as Anjali was concerned. The schedule was very hectic. So much so that there was hardly any spare time for reading or catching up with some literature which interested her. She still didn't get much time with Sunil at home, but now she felt as if Sunil didn't mind and this would put her off even more.

Chikitsa and Safdarjung hospitals were poles apart. *Chikitsa* catered for the elite who lived in and around Delhi's posh Vasant Vihar. Subsequently, Anjali kept having the nagging feeling that a large number of the symptoms of the patients were contrived, and somehow she didn't get the same satisfaction that she got at Safdarjung.

And so when Dr Yogi suggested that she take study leave to do her MD she jumped at the opportunity.

Three years after her marriage, Anjali got back to AIIMS to do her MD. She had got into the course quite easily, with the reputation that she had acquired and with the hard study that she put in. When her admission was announced, the first thing that she did was to go to Safdarjung hospital. There was a small party at Sunayana's room in the hospital. Sunayana was elated. She had finished her MD before she had joined Safdarjung Hospital and she was proud to have guided Anjali into AIIMS and into an MD in Medicine.

"Two years, and you'll be a medical specialist! Just imagine!" said Sunayana excitedly.

In contrast, the reaction at home was different.

"Does it make a difference to your career?" asked Sunil.

"Of course it does. I'll get better cases and I'll be able to do so much more for patients," said Anjali.

"No, what I mean is, will your pay increase substantially enough for you to waste two years?"

"Come off it Sunil, how can you call studies a waste of two years?" Anjali protested.

This time Anjali stood her ground and insisted on going through with the course.

Expectedly, Anjali did well in her MD examinations. This in spite of realising that she was pregnant a month after she joined up at the AIIMS. An exception had to be made in her case and she continued with the course after a tacit understanding with her dean that she would do her level best not to let the pregnancy interfere with her studies.

Halfway through her course, she gave birth to a baby boy. The Sharma household erupted with spontaneous joy. It was as if an unseasonal *Diwali* had been declared in their house. Ajay and Devika had no children of their own, but even then Devika took charge of things as if it was her own child.

"We'll call him Karan," she declared with an air of finality that no one would question. "Karan Sharma."

The initial few months were a period which Anjali would never forget. Alternating between the demands of Karan and her studies was not easy, but Anjali was determined not to be found lacking in either of them.

Chanda, a young woman of about twenty was employed by them for looking after the baby. On top of it Devika insisted on taking time off from the shop so that she could be nanny to Karan.

"I too need a break. Let Ajay and Sunil look after the business. You and I will look after the baby," she said.

It suited Anjali fine and this way she was able to give a lot of time to her studies.

6

By the time Karan was six months old, the novelty of the new child in the household seemed to have worn-off to an extent. When Karan started sitting up, Devika decided to go back to the shop. Slowly things settled down to the same old routine in the house. In a way, Anjali was glad. For the last six months she had always been told what to do and how it should be done. Now that she was alone with Karan in her spare time, she felt more like a mother.

In the routine of the Sharma house, Karan's illness went unnoticed for some time. It all started with a runny nose and since Karan was prone to catching colds frequently, no one took much notice of it. He had a mild fever and Anjali was treating it with Paracetemol. But when it didn't go away for four days and Karan started developing a high pitched cough, she got a bit worried.

"Karan has been coughing a lot in the night," she told Sunil.

"Is it?" said Sunil. "I didn't realise."

"You get so tired that you sleep like a log," said Anjali. "I want to take him to a pediatrician."

"Come on Anjali," said Sunil. "You're a doctor. I'm sure your treatment will be as good."

"No. I'll be happier if I show him at the hospital. I think I'll take him to Dr. Munshi today."

"Not today, Anjali," said Sunil, about to rush off to work. "I'm taking the car today. I have a lot of running around to do. And Ajay Bhaiya and *Bhabi* are taking theirs."

"Sunil, you didn't tell me beforehand. Suppose I had to go for classes today?"

"There's lots of work that has come up suddenly. You could take a day off from your classes today."

"And what about Karan?" asked Anjali.

"Won't tomorrow do?"

But then, seeing the worried look on her face, he came to her and sat down.

"Why don't you take Karan to the doctor at the beginning of the block. I've seen his board. He's a child specialist. Dr. Aakash Anand, I think his name is. You can walk down with Karan."

"Yes, I think I'll do that. Why don't you come with me?"

"I'm getting late, Anjali. You take Chanda along with you," said Sunil as he left.

Dr. Anand confirmed her suspicion almost immediately.

"It's a typical case of Pertussis - Whooping Cough," he said after examining the baby. "We'll start him on Erythromycin immediately. Come along, let's weigh him so that we can decide on the dosage."

He wrote out the prescription and handed it to her.

"Give this to him four times a day for five days and then let's have a look again," said Dr. Anand.

When she went back to him after five days, the effect of the medicine was already evident. This time there were no other patients waiting and so she introduced herself as his neighbour.

"Mrs. Sharma!" he said. " My father and I have been thinking of visiting all our neighbours since we moved in here six months ago, but somehow we never got down to it. Please call me Aakash."

He held out his hand to her.

"I'm Anjali," she said, instantly liking him.

When she told him that she too was a doctor, she could sense that their conversation would carry on for some time.

"Lovely," he said. "And where do you work?"

"Chikitsa Hospital."

"The one at Vasant Vihar?" he asked.

Anjali thought she could see him wrinkling his nose in distaste.

"Yes, have you been there?"

"I have. Just the once. I thought it looked more like a hotel than a hospital. Anyway, with Dr. Yogi, one could expect that."

"How come you know Dr. Yogi?" asked Anjali.

Aakash chuckled.

"We've done our medicine from the same college - Medical College of Georgia. Of course, he finished some fifteen years before I did. But since then, he's had the reputation of being more of an administrator than a doctor."

Anjali merely smiled. She couldn't have agreed more.

"And you, Anjali? Do you also plan to go into the glitzy world of showbiz medicine or are you planning some serious work?"

"Oh no," she said immediately.

And when she told him that she was doing her MD in internal medicine and that she planned to do as much research as she could, she could sense that their conversation would carry on much longer than she initially thought.

It would have - if young Karan was interested in the world of medicine. Right then he was more worried about the prospects of losing his next feed of Lactogen and so he used the only line of defence known to him.

He started bawling.

The next time they met was a few days later when Aakash dropped in for a cup of coffee after dinner.

"I came across to see my patient," he told Sunil when he opened the door. "I'm Dr. Anand. How's the young man?"

"Oh, he's fine. Come on in," said Sunil.

Devika and Ajay joined them in the drawing room. It was a boisterous one hour as Aakash talked non-stop and had them all in splits of laughter as he told them about anecdotes of some of his patients from the nearby hutments.

"There was this lady who came in with her one year old son with fever and rashes and when I told her that the child had chicken pox, she was aghast and she says ' but doctor we're vegetarians!'. I had no answer to that!"

Their manservant, Bahadur, came in with coffee and Anjali poured it out for all of them.

"Why do you accept patients from the hutments?" asked Ajay. "They would hardly be able to pay you for your time."

"Time." said Aakash, as he sipped his coffee. "Oh well that's one thing I have plenty of - twenty four hours in a day. And money - well sometimes I end up giving them money for buying medicines, instead of taking my fees from them."

Devika passed around some cake, which Aakash politely declined.

"Tell me Aakash. I hope I can call you Aakash." Devika carried on without waiting for a reply. "Why did Karan get Whooping Cough. He was vaccinated for it. Are these vaccines not genuine, or what?"

"No, Devika. I hope I can call you that." Anjali suppressed a smile as Aakash, too, carried on without waiting for a reply. "The traditional whooping cough vaccines were made from killed whole cell Pertussis bacteria. These would cause side effects - fever, irritability and swelling. Lately in use are cellular vaccines. These are made of only parts of the killed bacterial cells."

The repulsion on Devika's face was obvious.

"So in some very rare cases a patient gets affected in spite of the vaccine." Anjali finished the explanation.

As he was leaving, he turned to Anjali.

"How often do you go to AIIMS, nowadays?" he asked.

"Almost every day," said Anjali.

"Then could I take a lift with you for the next few days? I'm a consultant there. I go there in the mornings and my jeep is down with the mechanic for a week or so."

"Oh yes. Of course," said Anjali. "I'll pick you up at eight in the morning?"

"I'll be ready."

Over the next few days, the conversations that Anjali and Aakash had were a heady mix of topics ranging from the profession they shared, to things of daily life. To Anjali, the minutes they shared seemed to be packed with information and knowledge. They seemed to be minutes where she was learning about life from the beginning.

"Where are you headed for?" asked Aakash, one day.

Aakash had this knack of being able to jump from one topic to another so rapidly, that Anjali found it difficult to keep pace.

"Wh —what?" asked Anjali.

"Where are you headed for?" Aakash repeated himself.

"Home. I think," said Anjali hesitantly.

"No. No. In life, I mean," said Aakash. "Where are you headed for in life?"

"I don't know," said Anjali. "I don't think I've really given any thought to that question.

"Then aren't you just drifting - and not living? Can one get to any place unless one knows where the place is, in the first place?" asked Aakash.

"But why not play things by the ear?" asked Anjali.

"It won't work, unless you have an aim in life," mused Aakash. "Think of life like an airline flight. The captain does a lot of meticulous planning before he gets on board. He doesn't say 'I haven't given a thought as to where I'm headed'. He knows his destination. He draws up route maps. He knows the points enroute, to an extent that he is prepared for them. He knows what kind of opposition to expect on the way - opposition in the form of, maybe weather, maybe mechanical problems. And he thinks of how he'll get over them. Most importantly, he plans his diversions - he knows where and how to go to an alternate destination in case the main is not achievable!"

"Okay, if it's all that easy to put into words, what's your aim in life?" asked Anjali.

"Well, to make this world a better place to live in!" said Aakash immediately.

"Oh, and how do you think you'll do it?"

"I won't be able to do it. I'll only contribute to it," said Aakash. "If I can put a smile on the faces of even ten people, I would be very happy. And if everyone thought the same way, the world would be such a lovely place to live in. And now if you pull up to the side, I'll probably put a smile on my father's face for having got home early!"

"Whoops," said Anjali. "I didn't realise we've reached!"

Aakash got out of the car.

"Why don't you come in for a while? I make lovely coffee."

"I don't mind," said Anjali. "In fact, I think I need it."

This was the first time that she had actually gone into his house. The previous two visits had only been in and out of the clinic. What struck her at once was the atmosphere of academics and of art in the house. There was no pretense of style or of a display of wealth, things which she associated with her own house. There was just comfort all around. Comfort in the quietness, comfort in the books all around, comfort in the objects of art all around, comfort in the paintings all around.

Aakash let her absorb all of it before he spoke.

"Come, let me introduce you to my father," said Aakash as he led her into the next room.

They had tiptoed in so quietly that his father didn't even look up as they came into his work room. Anjali looked at him, almost mesmerised by his personality and by his work.

Mr. Anand was a very tall man. He was in his sixties and he would never try to hide even a year of it. His beard was white and so was the thick bush of hair on his head. He wore an apron as he carried on painting the portrait he was so intent on. He was working on the eyes of the almost complete painting and Anjali stood silently looking on and feeling as if the eyes were full of life and were looking at her.

Aakash saw her watching his father paint, dumbstruck, and suddenly he realised that he had been looking at her, gaping as a teenager might, at a very beautiful woman. For that was what he found her to be then!

He quickly looked away.

When he came back with coffee for the three of them, he found that Anjali and his father had introduced themselves - something which he should have done, but which he didn't in his confusion.

Now the two of them were busy discussing a stroke which he had put on the eyebrows of the lady which he was painting. In just those few moments that he had been away, the two of them had built up a rapport as if they both had been painting for years.

"And Anjali has probably never discussed painting ever before with anyone," thought Aakash to himself.

Anjali looked up at him and beamed.

"I've been discussing painting with Uncle," she said. "And you know what, Aakash, I've probably never discussed painting ever before with anyone."

The coffee seemed redundant.

Aakash joined the discussion, and for the next half hour they dissected the lady on the canvas to an extent that if anyone had cared to measure, the lady must probably have shifted a few inches, discomforted by the attention that she was getting.

"Why do you paint so many portraits?" asked Anjali.

"The word 'portrait' came from portrayal of traits," said Mr. Anand. "What better way of painting characters!"

Anjali looked imploringly at Aakash.

"Is that how the word came about?"

"Don't be silly," said Aakash. "It'll take you some time to catch on to his fast ones."

They laughed. And they drank the coffee which Aakash had made. And then they laughed some more.

It wasn't too long before the two of them - Aakash and his father became a hit in the normally sober Sharma family. Actually, it was the senior Anand who made more of an impact.

"Hello, Mr. Anand," said Devika as she welcomed him for dinner one night. "I didn't know we had a MF Hussain living next door to us."

He beckoned her close to him and then whispered in her ear. "I didn't know that Madhuri Dixit lived so close to me!"

After that Devika was all his for the rest of the evening. And when Mr. Anand announced that his next portrait was going to be one of Devika, she was his for the rest of her life!

Aakash's jeep took abnormally long to come out of the mechanic's garage. When it did come out, the two of them decided to continue going together in a car pool so as not to waste petrol.

"This thing! I'm going to travel in this thing?" asked Anjali when Aakash came to pick her up. She turned to Sunil, who was trying very hard to suppress his laughter.

Aakash gave a mock look of being very hurt.

The 'thing' that Anjali had referred to was Aakash's jeep. The Sharma's had two Maruti Esteems and somehow she had been expecting Aakash to drive up in something of that sort. The sight of a red 1970s Jeep put her off gear.

"All it needs is polka dots!" she announced.

Aakash stroked his chin in thought.

"Lovely idea. That'll be my next project," he said. "Black polka dots or yellow?"

"Don't you dare! This is bad enough," Anjali retorted. "Now let's go!"

That day Anjali got over with her classes at around noon. She gave a ring to Aakash and found that he had almost finished with all the patients in the OPD.

"Shall we have lunch together somewhere before setting course for home?" asked Anjali.

When they set off, Aakash had decided to take her to a place he used to frequent in his childhood.

"You're fond of Mughlai food, so I'm going to take you to a place called Gali Kababiyan," said Aakash. "My father used to take me there quite often because he was very fond of the feeling that he would get of being in an age gone by.

Aakash drove through the crowded roads of Delhi and reached the other end of the city.

They had a leisurely stroll down the crowded streets around the Jama Masjid in the old city of Delhi. The wonderful aroma of the tandoori dishes of Meena Bazaar made Anjali's mouth water. Meena Bazaar has a row of small shops, catering essentially for tourists. There are a lot of them selling trinkets, and Aakash immediately got interested in them.

"Aakash I'm hungry," pleaded Anjali.

Aakash led her into a by-lane and into Karim Hotel, where they dug into a hearty meal of *Kadhai* Chicken, a dish cooked in an open vessel over a slow fire. They ate it along with *Naan* – served hot and crisp, straight from the *Tandoor*. They had ordered a dish of *Shahi Paneer*- cooked along with a lot of dry fruits, in a very rich curry- but this didn't get the attention it deserved because of the chicken.

As they ate, Aakash told her that the restaurant was owned by a family that prides itself for having cooked delicacies for Bahadur Shah Zafar, the last Mughal emperor. The restaurant had now been running for over ninety years.

"Will you have some desert?" he asked.

"I don't know. I'm bursting. I'll probably share something with you," said Anjali.

They ended with *firni* - it had been set in individual earthenware dishes, and a mild taste of the earth had seeped into it.

When they finished, they sauntered down to Jama Masjid.

"Do you know, Anjali, this is the largest mosque in Asia," said Aakash as he took over the role of a guide to her. "It was Shahjahan's final contribution to Mughal architecture."

"When was it built?" asked Anjali.

"Sometime in the 1660s. In fact it was started by Shahjahan, but completed by Aurangzeb!"

They found the *Maulvi Sahib* and sat chatting with him for a while. He told them that the mosque was basically built as a Friday mosque, and its courtyard was so huge that it could house the entire population that turned up for the prayers in those days.

They sat quietly for some time after he left, taking in the beauty of the architecture, the bulbous domes, the minarets and the perfectly balanced structure.

"Shall we go?" said Anjali finally, quite reluctant to break the spell of fascination with which both of them sat. "It's getting late."

As they were coming out of the mosque, they had to cross a small open drain. Aakash held out his hand to her. He saw her hesitate for a while. And then they looked at each other and smiled. She held his hand and crossed over quite easily.

When they reached Anjali's house it was getting to be dark.

"Aakash …," said Anjali.

"What?"

"I just wanted to tell you that I had a wonderful time. I feel as if I've unwound myself. Thanks."

"Can I have something in return?" asked Aakash.

"What?"

"Can we do this again sometime?"

Anjali just looked at him and gave a mischievous grin.

"Anytime," she said. "Anytime that you feel like a Mughal emperor, I'll be willing to share your frugal meal!"

7

The first showdown between Devika and Anjali took place unexpectedly. It was a Sunday morning and everyone was at home.

"Anjali, the plumber will be coming tomorrow. You can show him the leaks in the kitchen."

"*Bhabi*, I've got a test tomorrow. I won't be able to skip class. I'll tell Bahadur to supervise," said Anjali.

"That, even I could do. But no, it's a long pending job and I want you to be around. Ask your professor to take a test for you some other time."

"But that's not possible. Nobody will take a test only for me."

"Call up and tell them that you are down with fever," suggested Devika.

"But that's not true. How can I possibly lie to a professor?"

"Oh come on, a professor isn't God's own shit. Don't make them sound like something out of this world. They're just like one of us. They work for the money in the job - that's it!" said Devika.

"You're wrong out there," said Anjali, losing her cool. "Teaching is a very noble profession and most professors are there because they enjoy teaching. They would still be around even if their pays were reduced!"

"You will never understand. All you want to do is what comes to your mind, without thinking of our family and our needs," Devika said as she stormed out of the room.

In a rage herself, Anjali too, stormed out of the room and went into her room with Sunil following.

"Take it easy, Anjali," he said. "Don't make such a big issue of a small thing."

"Small thing, Sunil? You call that a small thing? She never tries to understand my point of view. It's always her point of view which we must follow."

"But she's probably right. You need to concentrate a bit more on the family. You spend more time with your books than with the household chores," said Sunil.

Anjali stared at him in disbelief.

"You never spoke like that to me before we got married," she said. "You said all that mattered was me. Where do mundane things like household chores come into it?"

"That's part of life, Anjali."

"Well, knowledge is part of my life," said Anjali, picking up Karan from his cot. "And it's going to be part of Karan's life too!"

Sunil snatched Karan away from her. "Karan is going to be part of my business as soon as he grows up. Let's be clear on that."

With her eyes brimming with tears, Anjali went out of the house and started walking away, not aware of where she was going. Suddenly she realised that she was in front of Aakash's house. She went in and almost ran into his clinic from inside the house. That's where she knew he would be.

Aakash was busy with a patient and across the screen Anjali could see that there were another six or seven patients waiting with their little kids. She turned to go away, but Aakash had seen her.

"Hi Anjali, what's up?" he asked.

"Nothing, I think I'll come later."

"No, sit in my room. I'll just be with you."

Anjali, lost in her thoughts walked into his room and sat in the midst of the typical chaos of a bachelor's room. She was already feeling a lot better when Aakash finished with his patient and came looking for her.

"Aakash, I'm sorry barging in like this..."

He looked at her. "You've been crying, Anjali! What happened?"

"Nothing. Just a speck of dust in my eye, I think."

"Bullshit, Anjali. You think I don't know you? Sit down and start from the beginning. "

"Aakash it's just some silly discussions in the house. It wouldn't interest you."

This time there was a sternness in his voice. "Anjali, I want to know," he said very slowly.

All of a sudden Anjali started crying. She sat on his bed and tears rolled down her cheeks. Aakash pulled up a chair and sat across her. He just sat quietly for a while and let her cry. Anjali put her head down in her hands and as she did, her long hair spilled down the side. Once again, Aakash found his thoughts wandering. This time, not only did he find her looking beautiful, but he felt like reaching out to her and wiping the tears off her cheeks. He felt like reaching out to her and holding her head to his chest and letting her cry as much as she wanted. He felt like going and sitting on the bed beside her and putting his arms around her.

All he did, instead, was to keep sitting quietly till she looked up.

"I'm sorry, Aakash," said Anjali.

"Don't be. Just go across to my bathroom and wash your face."

When she came back, Aakash was still sitting in the same chair.

"I'm really very sorry, Aakash."

"If you don't mind could you please tell me what's happened? I'm rather blank."

Anjali started right at the beginning - of her expectations from her marriage - of her expectations in her profession.

"Somehow, things seem to be going all haywire," she said. "Everything appeared so rosy before marriage and now it all seems to have settled down into a monotonous routine. I can almost predict the conversations that would take place every day in the house."

Aakash listened to her for a long time. He looked at her with a half smile on his face as he watched the intensity on her face as she talked on.

"Tell me, Aakash, do you think I made a mistake in my marriage?" asked Anjali suddenly.

"Whoa, Anjali, hold it, hold it," said Aakash. "Don't jump to such drastic conclusions. Sometimes our perceptions get clouded by one odd incident. Don't let that happen. Everyone has a point of view and lots of times these differ from ours. So think rationally and only then decide who was right and who was wrong."

"I don't know. I just feel like running away from it all," said Anjali.

"But is that a mature response?" asked Aakash. "Aren't you at fault to some extent too? Don't you need to be a part of their household and to share the odd jobs in the house?"

"Aakash, that's not the point. It's not as if I haven't been doing my bit. It's just that I'm not regarded by them as being important. Again it's not that there is a crunch for money. If that was the case, then my attitude would have been different. Somehow they feel that I should just give up my studies and live life the way they do. If I give up my profession and join their business, everything would be okay. Now you tell me, should I do that?"

"No, Anjali. I wouldn't even tell you to think about it. You get to live life only once. Live life from your heart. Do what feels best to you. Do what gives you the most satisfaction - because it is in that that you would excel. Einstein did what gave him the most satisfaction and see what he achieved. If he had become a tailor just because his mother-in-law wanted him to be one, then you probably wouldn't even have heard his name."

They laughed and all at once, the seriousness of the situation eased off.

"I better get going before a search party comes looking for me," said Anjali as she got up to leave. "Why don't you come across for lunch. I'll make some lovely *Biryani* for you."

"Sure, I'd love it," said Aakash without hesitating.

After lunch, Aakash and Sunil lit up cigarettes and went into the living room. Anjali joined them there.

"Sunil, why don't both of you come along with me. I've got to go to Karol Bagh to pick up a saree for my aunt. I'm lousy at these things, so you can help," said Aakash.

"Not on a Sunday afternoon," said Sunil. "I'd much prefer a nap. Why don't you take Anjali along. In any case she'll be a better judge than me."

When they drove off an hour later, Anjali turned to Aakash. "Which aunt of yours is this?"

"Anjali, I don't have an aunt. My Papa, too, was an only child."

Anjali turned to look at him and he grinned back at her.

"I just wanted to chat a little more with you."

"And what if someone at my place asks you about your aunt?" asked Anjali.

"I'll just say that she died of shock when she saw the saree that Anjali had chosen for her."

"Aakash, you are quite a clown!"

Over the next few weeks, Anjali found herself being drawn close to Aakash. Sometimes she would think of the fact that she might regret it later, but she desperately needed a friend. She desperately needed an emotional outlet and she found most of it all in Aakash. She started going to him for the littlest advice that she might need, whether in her studies or in her day to day life. She found solace in being able to pour out her problems to him. He, on his part, was gentle and patient with her. He seemed to be there whenever she wanted help.

"Soul mate, shall I call you?" she asked him one day.

All he did was to lean across and hold her hand. He squeezed it gently and Anjali closed her eyes. A kaleidoscope of emotions was going through her and she didn't know how to react.

"Don't be so nice to me, Aakash," she said at last. "Don't be so nice to me that I drift away from others."

"How come you took up Pediatrics," asked Anjali, one day.

"Oh, well. First of all," said Aakash "I love children and secondly, I love detective stories. For years, I would be intrigued by stories where a guy pieced together clues from here and there and then solved a mystery. It's like that in Pediatrics."

"Aakash, you can't be serious," said Anjali.

"In fact, I am. A very small child's illness is like a mystery. Grown up patients at least come and tell their symptoms. Babies only bawl. Now I look for clues – the way they bawl, the way they look imploringly at you when you press their stomach which is bloated with colic! And, besides, I get along well with kids. It gives me a big kick when a bawling baby becomes quiet for a while when he is in my arms."

"But then, you're so good at your job," said Anjali. Look at me – I don't know how good I'll be when I become a medical specialist."

"No, Anjali," Aakash was unusually stern. The first thing that anyone needs in life is confidence – confidence in oneself. Confidence wins half the battle. People who doubt their own capabilities are losers. They lose before they even start. So don't be like that. In any case, you know you are good. You know you'll be better than the rest."

"I really do hope so," said Anjali.

"What'll you do when you finish your MD?" asked Aakash. "Will you get back to *Chikitsa?*"

"I don't know – I really don't know," said Anjali.

"What does your heart tell you to do?"

"My heart says – go back to Safdarjung Hospital. And I know the hospital would love to have me back. Sunayana told me so."

"Who's Sunayana?" asked Aakash.

"She's a colleague of mine – a Medical Specialist," said Anjali. "You must meet her and her husband one day. They're such a lovely couple."

"I had a chat about this with my father a few days back," Anjali continued, getting back to where she would want to work.

"What did he say?" asked Aakash.

"Oh, he's funny – he never gives any solid advice," said Anjali. "His advice is always the same – think, think and do what's best for you!"

"And …," Aakash coaxed her to continue.

"It's just that there are so many pressures on me," said Anjali.

"What kind of pressures?" Aakash was curious.

"Well, family pressure," said Anjali.

"Oh… I see," said Aakash.

"You tell me Aakash," said Anjali. "You tell me what I should do."

"Anjali, I think I know you pretty well now. I know you're not cut out for an establishment like *Chikitsa*. You'll be much happier and you'll find much more satisfaction in working at Safdarjung hospital. And that's what I think you should do."

"I guess you're right," said Anjali. "Okay, so that's what I'll do. Dr. Yogi will get quite a shock. But, I'm going back to what I love."

Anjali had quite a happy expression as they drove back home.

It was just a chance encounter with Sumitra at the parking lot of AIIMS.

"Sumitra," Anjali almost yelled out, "what are you doing out here?

They chatted for quite some time, while Aakash sat in the car and when they drove back, Anjali chatted about Sumitra for a while.

"She was my roommate during my first two years at AIIMS," said Anjali.

"As intelligent as you?" asked Aakash.

"No," Anjali laughed. "She was such a dodo – but fun to be with, all the same."

They drove silently for a while.

"We had become close friends in those two years," Anjali thought aloud. "You know, she used to call me Anju – somehow I used to like it. Nobody has ever used any name other than Anjali for me."

"Okay ma'am, I've got the point. I'll call you Anju from now on," Aakash teased.

"I'd love it," said Anjali.

The World Pediatric Conference for the year was being held in London. Aakash had been invited for it and he was looking forward to it.

"I'm presenting a paper on measures being taken to prevent typhoid fever amongst children in India. People the world over think that we not doing very much about it. They just don't realise the magnitude of the problem because of the population. And then, if other developed countries realise the enormity of the problem, we'll probably be able to generate some more funds for the programmes."

"Are you going to be talking about the need for education programmes, too?" asked Anjali.

"Yes, of course. It's only awareness which will help in improving sanitation conditions, especially in the villages," said Aakash.

"When do you get back?"

"Three weeks to be precise – there's an old family friend of ours in Manchester who's been insisting that I spend some time with them. I thought I'd do that this time."

"What time is your flight in the morning, Aakash?"

"I'm leaving home at six thirty - a day in Mumbai and then the next night to London."

"I'll take an early morning walk," said Anjali. "I'll see you off from here, so wait for me."

The next morning, Anjali overslept. She had told Sunil to wake her up, but he too overslept. When she got up, it was past seven. In a mad rush, she got out of bed and dialed Aakash's number. There was no response.

"Sunil, wake up. I want to go to the airport. I had promised Aakash that I would see him off," said Anjali shaking him up.

"Don't be ridiculous, Anjali," said Sunil. "By the time we get there, the flight would have taken off. In any case he'll be back in a couple of weeks. You can say sorry to him then."

Anjali felt a wave of emptiness sweeping through her. Very woodenly, she went to the kitchen and warmed a bottle of milk for Karan.

When she came back and sat on the bed, Sunil sensed her mood and came up to her.

"You're feeling bad, isn't it?" he asked as he put his arms around her. As he did, Anjali started crying.

"How could I do this?" Anjali was sniffing. "How could I do this to Aakash, of all people?"

"See, this is what happens when you become close to a friend. It's always best to keep a distance from everyone," said Sunil.

"No, I don't think that's right. It's a nice feeling, too," said Anjali.

An hour later, the telephone rang. Sunil picked it up. It was Aakash on the line.

"Aakash, where are you?" asked Sunil.

"I'm calling from the airport. I just thought I'd say bye."

"Here speak to Anjali. She's been crying away."

He handed the receiver to Anjali.

"Aakash, I'm terribly sorry. I got up late," said Anjali.

"Hey, don't be silly. I guessed so. That's why I called up to say bye."

"No, I was feeling bad," said Anjali.

"Anju, you've been crying?"

"No," said Anjali. "No, I'll be okay. I just have to go to the bathroom and wash my face…. Here you speak to Sunil."

When Aakash put the phone down, he kept thinking for a long time. He really didn't know whether his thoughts were very collected, or whether what he was about to do was the right thing or not. He was shaken out of his thoughts when an obese lady with bright red lipstick asked rather sarcastically if he had finished with the telephone.

"I'm sorry," he muttered, as he picked up his bag and headed towards the Air India counter.

"I'd like to change my flight, please," said Aakash as he pushed his ticket across the counter. "I'd like to leave tomorrow instead of today - the direct flight to London. I'll skip Mumbai."

He got off the taxi in front of Anjali's house. It was just past nine thirty and, expectedly, both cars were missing.

"Anjali must have gone to the Institute," he thought.

He walked in and rang the bell, nevertheless. And the delight on both their faces when Anjali opened the door was very obvious.

"Come on in," said Anjali, as she held Aakash's hand and pulled him in.

"How come you're at home?" asked Aakash.

"Would you believe me if I say that somehow I knew you'd come back?"

"But that's no reason for you to miss out at the Institute," said Aakash.

"*Bas, bas…*, enough of lecturing. Just sit quietly at the dining table. Bahadur has gone to buy vegetables and so I'm going to make you one of your favourite fluffy omelettes and crisp toasts to go with it. And some coffee?"

Nobody else was at home. Chanda was busy giving Karan a bath and so Aakash found himself in the kitchen chopping an onion.

"Aakash, watch the toasts...."

"Anju, flip the omellette or it'll burn ..."

"Oh God, I think I should have waited for the omellette to get done, before putting the coffee to boil."

"Switch it off, we'll have the coffee later."

"Pass me a plate, the omellette is done. Here you are, nice and golden brown!"

"Anju, I once watched the launch of a space mission on TV and well, I think there was a bit less confusion at the NASA Control Centre!"

Anjali whacked him with a napkin. "Aakash, don't be mean! I don't make omellettes every day. Now sit down and eat your breakfast - and say it's lovely."

Aakash pulled up a chair and sat on the small dining table in the kitchen itself.

"How is it?" asked Anjali as she watched him dig into the egg.

"You said to say it was nice," said Aakash.

"Idiot, not that way."

"Okay, seriously it's lovely," said Aakash. 'But, now that the panic is over, can I ask you a simple question – what did you make me chop that onion for?"

Anjali's mouth fell open. "You mean – God! – I forgot the onions!"

They burst out laughing – and they kept laughing until Aakash realised that Anjali had tears in her eyes when she stopped laughing.

"Anju ...?"

"I'm so sorry Aakash, I'm really very sorry. Your programme got upset because of me," said Anjali.

"Don't be," said Aakash. "In fact, I've never felt so important before. Now you get ready quickly while I leave my bag at home and pick up my jeep. Then I'll take you to AIIMS, for you to try and catch up.

For the first one week after he left, there was no call from Aakash. Whichever room she was in, Anjali would be all ears whenever the telephone rang. Routine business calls, calls from some colleagues at *Chikitsa*, even a couple of calls from Sunayana – suddenly everything seemed so mundane. Whenever there was a call for her, Anjali would make sure she kept the conversation short, so that if Aakash was trying to call, the telephone wouldn't be engaged.

"Just six months, I've known him," thought Anjali, "and in six days I'm missing him as if he's been around for years."

Anjali found herself living with two time zones in her mind. London would be five and a half hours behind – so when she was having lunch at the AIIMS students' cafeteria, she would think of the *croissants* that Aakash must be having for breakfast.

When she came out of the cafeteria, one of the other students told her that the final exam timetable was up on the notice board. Anjali went across to note it down. Just two weeks left. A week of exams and then it would all be over.

"Let's go out for dinner," suggested Sunil when she got back home.

"No Sunil, my exams are just two weeks away. I've got to study."

"Oh! Come on, I know you'll do well without even touching your books," said Sunil. "Why don't you do some reading early in the morning instead of at night?"

But Anjali insisted on staying behind, while Sunil, Ajay and Devika went out to Pandara Road for dinner. It wasn't just studies that made her stay behind. It was also the fact that nine thirty in the night meant four in the evening in London – and that Aakash might call up.

He did. It was just past eleven when the phone rang.

"See, sixth sense," said Anjali. "I knew you'd call up today. It's been so many days since you went. You know I'd want to talk to you. Why didn't you call up earlier?"

"Hey give me a chance," Aakash cut her monologue short. "No, no reason at all. It's just that I thought it might look odd if I call up and if someone else had picked up the phone. I wouldn't have known what to talk about."

"How did the conference go?" asked Anjali.

"Oh, my presentation went off very well," said Aakash. "There were so many responses that ultimately the moderator had to intervene. You tell me about your studies."

"Aakash, you're going to find this very silly and probably childish – but …" Anjali paused.

"But what ..?"

"Aakash, can you skip Manchester and come back. My final exams start two weeks from now, and … well, just your being around would be quite a moral support."

"Anju… behave yourself," was all that Aakash said.

Aakash's flight landed at the Indira Gandhi International Airport, at exactly midnight the next night. Just after the conversation with Anjali, he called up the airlines office, but that was the earliest flight to which he could advance his ticket.

Anjali's exams went off very well. In fact, they went off much better than she expected.

"I'll pick you up from outside your examination hall," Aakash had told her. He had tied up the programme a couple of days before the last exam. We'll go out for lunch and then I'll take you to a place, which I've been wanting to show you for a while.

"Where's that?" asked Anjali.

"Wait, it'll be a surprise. You do well in your exams and I'll look forward to it."

But, on the morning of the last exam, Sunil announced quite unexpectedly that he'd pick her up.

"And then we can go out and have lunch to celebrate," he said.

"Why do you want to take a day off?" Anjali tried to wriggle out of the situation. "Tomorrow's a Sunday – as it is your shop will be closed. So, let's go celebrate tomorrow."

"No," insisted Sunil. "Today's your last exam and you'll enjoy the celebration much more today itself. Don't take the car today. Go with Aakash in his jeep in the morning so that he can come back on his own."

On the way to the Institute, when Anjali told Aakash about the change in the plan, she sensed a sudden change in his mood. He was silent for most of the drive. Very close to the Institute, she squeezed his hand.

"Don't be upset, Aakash," she said. "We'll go out on Monday."

"I'm not upset, Anjali," Aakash lied. "It's just that I'm preoccupied with one of my patients who's admitted at the hospital."

"As if I don't know you," said Anjali. "I knew you'd be upset. But, I couldn't help it. Now be a good guy and wish me luck for my last exam."

"Yes, all the best," said Aakash. "Do well. You have to do well for your own sake."

The exam went off well, but the afternoon didn't. Sunil wanted to go to 'Drums of Heaven' – a Chinese restaurant in Green Park, but Anjali said no to that. It was Aakash's favorite place for Chinese and the two of them had gone there a couple of times. They went, instead, to another restaurant in Lajpat Nagar.

"You said that the exam went off well," said Sunil. "Then why are you so quiet today?"

"Am I?" asked Anjali. "No, I think I'm just a bit tired."

"You know," said Sunil scooping a spoonful of Chicken-in-garlic-sauce into his mouth, "I've been thinking of asking you for a while now. You've been very different in the last few months - sort of quiet, sort of lost. Is something bugging you?"

"Oh no, not at all," Anjali was toying with her food. "I think it's been the pressure of studies and then the thought of what I should do after I finish MD."

"Why, what's the doubt in your mind? You've already got such a nice job."

"It's just that… You know that I'm not too happy there," said Anjali, hesitantly. Sunayana was suggesting that I get back to Safdarjung."

"That Sunayana of yours!" Sunil showed his exasperation. "I don't think her advice means much. Hasn't Dr. Yogi promised you a raise after you finish MD?"

Two days later, when she met Aakash, he was back to his normal self. She had no work in the college, so she caught an auto to meet him after his OPD got over.

They discussed a four year old child who was admitted with pancreatitis. "It's very rare in children," said Aakash. "This little child has a biliary tract ascariasis."

"Has he started developing fever?" asked Anjali.

"Yes, it's developed since yesterday – about 102 degrees."

"His age will be on his side," said Anjali. "So don't worry so much about it."

"I wouldn't have," Aakash seemed quite worried, "but there are signs of atelectasis in the lower lobe of the lung and quite a bit of pleural effusion."

"Oh!" said Anjali.

They drove silently for a while, until Aakash suddenly looked up. "Shucks, I'm sorry – where should we go for lunch? I promised you lunch today – as a belated celebration."

"Let's just drive around a bit – beyond Qutub. Then we'll come back for lunch," said Anjali. "And don't call it belated. The actual celebration is today."

"Okay, ma'am"

"And don't 'ma'am' me," said Anjali. "I'm in quite a bitchy mood today."

"Let me draw you out of that," said Aakash. "Open the glove compartment – there's a poem I wrote for you today."

They were now on a quiet road leading towards housing colonies which were planned, but not yet built. Anjali pulled out the neatly folded white paper and read out aloud.

So often,
have we held hands and walked in the clouds.
So often,
have you rested your head on my shoulders and dreamt.

So often,
have you held me close as if never to let me go.
So often,
have I stroked your hair and got lost, deep in them.
So often,
have you cried in your pillow when you have missed me.
So often,
have I taken you to Venice just to be in the world of romanticism.
So often,
have we drifted in a boat through the rivers of the city.
So often,
have you slept in my arms as the boatsman hummed a soft song.
So often,
have you kissed me in the moonlight - soft, lingering, lost to the world.
So often,
have I lived in my personal, private world of fantasy ......!

They fell quiet again for a while as Aakash turned the jeep around.

"Aakash, hold my hand," Anjali said it in almost a whisper and Aakash didn't catch on.

"What?"

"Hold my hand, you idiot!" hissed Anjali.

He held her hand softly at first and then their fingers entwined, and talked to each other, as if their vocal chords had temporarily shifted down from their throats to their hands. Aakash drove on, with one hand, for a while. When the traffic started building up, Aakash spoke up.

"Anju, there's something I have to tell you."

Anjali didn't respond.

"Don't you want to ask me what?" asked Aakash.

"I know what it is," said Anjali, very hesitatingly. "I don't want to hurt you, Aakash, but I'm committed to Sunil."

"Yes, I know," was all that Aakash said.

"You're brooding again," said Anjali. "I've hurt you, haven't I?"

"Hey look, look," Aakash yelled suddenly. "Look at that fat lady! She reminds me of a teacher of mine who went to the tailor to get a dress made. You know, the tailor while measuring her girth put one end of the measuring tape on her tummy and said 'You hold this here ma'am, I'll just come' and then he went around her with the other end of the tape."

They both laughed and the tension evaporated.

"Let's go to 'Drums of Heaven' for Chinese," suggested Anjali.

"But you had Chinese just two days back," said Aakash.

"But that wasn't with you."

They had quite a sumptuous meal. It was well beyond lunch time and both of them were very hungry. The meal started with a clear Chicken Coriander soup and went on to Hong Kong Chicken and Hakka Noodles. To polish it off, Anjali asked for some Chinese tea.

"Wow, that was lovely!" said Anjali, patting her tummy.

As they were going out, there was the usual tray with cellophane wrapped single roses. The *Durban* always offered one to each lady as she would leave. As he did so to Anjali, Aakash butted in and took the rose.

"Excuse me! Can I do the honours please," said Aakash, offering the rose to Anjali. And then he turned to the *Durban* and said "Nobody, but me, gives a rose to my lady!"

The stiff *Durban* was visibly quite perplexed.

On their way back, Anjali insisted on going to the place that Aakash had planned to take her after her last exam.

"Okay, but we'll have to rush through. I've got to get back for my clinic," said Aakash.

"Where are we going?" asked Anjali.

"It's a place lots of people in Delhi have heard of but never been to. The culture in Delhi is either to go to a place where one can have a picnic or where one can have a meal. Or then, of course, people go to temples, where they can offer a few rupees or some sweetmeats and ask for miracles in return. Most people go to temples and ask for happiness for themselves. But if you ask them what they mean by 'happiness' – they get quite foxed. So I'm taking you to a temple where there are no deities -where the only God is you, and where, if you want something, you have to ask for it from yourself."

When they took off their shoes, just before entering the Baha'I temple, both of them stood outside looking in awe at the structure. It was as if they were fascinated by the impression they got of a half-open lotus flower, afloat on water, surrounded by its leaves. It hardly looked like a traditional temple. It looked more like some sort of architectural wonder.

"Fariburz Sahiba was the architect who designed this," whispered Aakash. "His intention was to make something which would be loved by people of all religions."

"Wow, Aakash," said an enthralled Anjali, as they walked barefoot on the curved balustrades around the structure. "I had seen pictures of this so many times, but I've never come here before!"

"There's a big hall in the centre, with benches," said Aakash. "You can sit quietly out there for as long as you want. When you enter, you'll find that the hall itself is very cool. That's because there are openings at the basement and at the top, and the design is such that the warm air in the hall is drawn up and expelled from the top – somewhat like a chimney."

They entered the central hall of worship. Natural light filtered through the inner folds of the structure. Once again Aakash whispered to her, telling her that the central bud of the structure is held by nine open petals, each of which functions as a skylight.

They sat quietly on a bench in one corner, each lost in thought, each talking to the inner God within oneself. And when Anjali finally broke the spell by reaching out for Aakash's hand, both of them seemed so much at peace with themselves.

"You know what I asked for?" Anjali whispered to Aakash. "I just hoped that you'll be with me for the rest of my life."

"I guess it was the same with me," said Aakash.

"Let's go now!" Anjali said.

8

It was as if she was postponing the crisis. Her leave from *Chikitsa* was to end in ten days. She went across to her parents' place and talked for hours with her father.

"You have to do some soul searching," he said. "Whenever faced with a dilemma, look within yourself. You'll always find the answers there."

"But it's like a multiple choice question for me," protested Anjali. "I've searched within myself, but every time I come up with more than one answer."

"You've done so many exams, *beta*," her father said. "You know that there's got to be just one answer which will get you the top score."

"Why can't there be a choice like 'all of the above'?"

Aakash, on the other hand, was absolutely sure that leaving *Chikitsa* and getting back to Safdarjung would be the best for her. In fact, he seemed to think that that was a foregone conclusion.

"Always do what makes you happy," was what he always insisted on.

At home, the thought process was different. Anjali wasn't sure at all of the kind of reaction she would get – and so she rarely spoke about it. She knew that Sunil wanted her to get back to *Chikitsa* – but she wasn't sure why. She sensed that he enjoyed the eliteness associated with a doctor working in that hospital – something which she herself wasn't too comfortable with.

Anjali looked at her watch. It was eleven in the morning, the time that Aakash took his usual coffee break from the OPD. She dialed his number and had a chat with him.

"The last couple of days have been so nice," she told him. "I've managed to spend so much time with Karan."

"And with yourself?"

"Yes, and lots of time with myself. It's been great!"

"Can I intrude into your time," suggested Aakash. "Dad has taken his paintings for an exhibition, so I'll be having lunch all alone at home. Join me?"

"Yes, okay," said Anjali.

"I'll pick up some burgers on the way – and bring Karan with you when you come."

Anjali thought they'd end up discussing her problem when they met. But somehow, they drifted on to the topic of marriage. It was her question, actually, which started it.

"You've never really discussed this before, Aakash," she said, laying out the plates on the table. "Why is it that you never got married?"

Aakash had a big, mischievous grin on his face.

"Because by the time I found you, you were already married!"

"Well, why don't you propose to me even now?" she shot back.

Aakash became serious. "Are you nuts? Marriage is a very serious thing. It's a 'commitment', like you said. Didn't you see – just that one word made me realize a lot of things."

Anjali pulled out two cokes from the fridge. "No, but actually you're probably wrong. I've also been thinking. When I used that word, I didn't mean that I could never break that commitment."

"Don't be silly, Anju. How can you even think like that? Marriage is like a very big, one time investment."

Anjali bit thoughtfully into her burger. "So is buying a house. It's a very big, one time investment. You might be fascinated by it externally – but once you start living in it, you might end up pretty much dissatisfied. It just might not meet your needs. You might feel claustrophobic in it. It might be dull and dreary, however much you might do to spruce it up. What do you do then? Keep tolerating it because it's a onetime investment? Won't you move on to something to your likes?"

"I don't think that's a very good example, Anju," said Aakash. "You can't just equate marriage with buying a house."

"Why not? You live in both, don't you?"

Aakash reached for the French fries which he had picked up along with the burgers. He spoke with his mouth full. "You've got to understand that if two people live together, they are bound to have a bit of turbulence. Some conflict exists in all relationships. I'm sure if you were married to me, even we would have had our ups and downs."

"Mister Aakash Anand – are you trying to be obscene?"

"Oh Gosh, no – the pun was absolutely unintended!"

Anjali wasn't too sure, but she continued. "It's not a question of conflicts. That's possible to get across. It's the whole scenario of the setup at home. That household lives differently. They don't believe in thinking individually. They don't believe in even a bit of privacy of thought. In fact, there's always such a lot of commotion in that house that I wonder how I manage to think at all. Sunil never told me all this before our marriage."

Aakash had finished his burger and found that he was still hungry. He went across to the fridge and pulled out some bread and cheese. He brought a knife and sat down to make a sandwich for himself.

Anjali carried on, quite engrossed in letting out her pent up thoughts. "Aakash I need space to live. I need place in my mind to let my thoughts grow. All that happens is that for so long now, my mind is just cluttered with mundane things."

"Now that's something I'll agree with you about," said Aakash. "So all you have to do is to find time for yourself."

"Very funny! That's the crux of the problem. It's very easy for you to say that, because the atmosphere in your house is so different."

Anjali had finished her coke and now she turned the bottle upside down as if she was amazed that a bottle of coke could get over so fast.

"Do you want some more?" asked Aakash.

"No, but give me a couple of sips of yours."

"Don't – there's an old ladies' belief that if you share food or a drink with someone, then your love for him will increase!"

Anjali pulled the bottle out of Aakash's hand. "Then I'm going to finish the whole bottle," she said defiantly.

Aakash laughed. "You know what, Anju, you're just being a defiant little child, who doesn't know how to handle a small situation."

"Small situation – hah!" Anjali banged the bottle on the table.

"You must remember that minor disappointments can be made to disappear if you learn to cope with them, rather than getting worked up over them," said Aakash.

"Minor disappointments – hah!" Anjali got up. "You'll never understand me, Aakash Anand. You live in your idealistic world. You never see reality even when it stares in your face – you'll see it only when it blows up in your face. See you, I'm going."

And Anjali stormed out of the house leaving Aakash to clear up the table. He sat, drumming his fingers on the table for a long time. Then he let out a sigh. He really wasn't sure whether Anjali had been dramatizing, or whether she was actually worked up.

He was wondering how he was going to spend the afternoon, when the telephone rang shrilly in the quiet house. It was Anjali. "I'll be ready in fifteen minutes. Pick me up. I want to go your Dad's painting exhibition."

Aakash started to talk into the phone, but before he could do so, he realized that she had already put her phone down. He smiled to himself and then went into his bedroom to change.

They spent an hour or so at the exhibition. Aakash's father was thrilled to see them. He was talking with a rich-looking couple, when he sighted Aakash and Anjali. He excused himself and came across to them.

"That's lovely," he said to Anjali. "I'm sure you must have convinced Aakash to come. This son of mine has no interest in art. You must ask him about his last painting. Let's see if he tells you. Normally he shies away from talking about it."

A very fair, elegant looking lady in her late fifties had just walked in. With a twinkle in his eye, Aakash's father strolled across to her.

"You must watch this, Anju," said Aakash. "Now Dad's charm will be all guns ablaze. I'll bet you a hundred, he'll clinch a deal with that lady."

"So that's where you've picked up your genes from!" said Anjali.

"Oh - You mean to say I do manage to charm people at times?"

Anjali had her eyebrows raised. She was about to answer when she stopped and only thought to herself, "I wish you knew, Aakash – I wish you knew just how much!"

"What was that about your last painting?" she asked, instead.

"Dad used to do such nice paintings that I used to keep trying to imitate him. I knew I used to keep failing, but the ultimate was when I once drew a cat. I thought it was quite okay, so I went running to him to collect my accolades. He did admire it. But with a puzzled look he had asked me 'Why is the trunk missing?' I stopped drawing after that!"

Anjali was laughing when Aakash nudged her. Aakash's father was shaking hands with the lady. Very obviously a deal had been struck. As he led the lady away to sign the papers, Mr. Anand turned towards Anjali and winked at her.

Aakash put his hand out to Anjali. "My hundred —?"

"*Chalo*, I'll treat you to cold coffee, instead."

Over the coffee, Anjali got back to the topic of marriage once again. It was as if it was pent up in her for so long that she wanted to let it out in one go.

"Anju, tell me – did someone force you into marriage?" asked Aakash. "You chose what you wanted. Then why crib about it now – after four years?"

"You've started off on your illogical logic again," said Anjali. "Well, maybe I made a mistake. Maybe I just kept looking at one facet of life with a man. I saw him and I got impressed – by the way he talked, by the way he walked – that's it!"

Aakash kept quiet as she spooned out some ice-cream from her glass of cold coffee, and let her continue with her monologue.

"Today when I look back, it's as if I'm looking at a grade card and seeing fabulous scores against one subject – and turning the grade card to see who it belongs to – because I'm fascinated by the score. So impressed am I that I don't even want to see anyone else's grade card – because who could do better? Some guy comes along and collects all the other grade cards, leaving me clutching the one I have – because I'm in an euphoric state of mind – who could be better? And then, much later, I look again at the grade card and realize that there are lots of other subjects and against most of them, the marks are so low that they are underlined in red. So what should I do – keep on being impressed by the same grade card?"

Anjali paused, still deep in thought. "So it's been with my marriage. I was very impressed with Sunil. It was only later that I realized how unimportant just that one aspect of a personality was to me. And you know what, you are responsible for this!"

"What? —— me?" Aakash looked up. "How—?"

"You showed me how to differentiate. You've sort of given a path to my thoughts. And I needed that. I needed to channelise my thinking to be able to move ahead. Why should I just accept anything as it happens?"

"Anju, you're living in a society. Some norms, some ways of life have to be followed. You don't want to be ostracized."

"Nothing like that will happen. I'm not just a housewife. I'm a professional and I can live alone. I can take Karan and go to America. So what if your society here says something to me. I'll move to another society and start life again. At least I'll be able to do what I want to."

"Anju, this is not what I ever meant to convey to you." Aakash was getting more and more flabbergasted. He wasn't sure at all of how to deal with the situation. "Whenever I've told you to move ahead, or to channelise your thoughts or to live from your heart, I've always been talking about your profession – and not of your personal life."

"I know," said Anjali. "But when a person's way of thinking changes, it changes across the spectrum. If I can sieve out the good from the not-so-good in my profession, then surely I can do it in my personal life first."

"Not like this, Anju."

"Then how? Just by sitting back and — and — what was that word you used — 'vegetating'? No Aakash – I'm going to get out of a mundane life – and from daily resentments – and from accumulated disappointments."

Aakash paid the bill and stood up. As they came out into the streets of Khan Market, they realized that their jeep was now wedged between two other cars. It took some time for Aakash to be able to get the jeep out. As it was, he was deep in thought as he was manipulating the jeep.

In most situations, Aakash was quite adept at being able to diffuse the seriousness. Somehow, wit was always at the tip of his tongue. At that moment, however, leave alone the tip, Aakash didn't really know where his tongue was.

About halfway back to Greater Kailash, Anjali was apologetic. "I'm sorry Aakash. I've carried on like a nagging wife today. Since lunch, I've only been talking about myself. You're bugged?"

"No, Anju. I'm not bugged," said Aakash. "But I think I'll tell you why I didn't marry."

Anjali shifted on the seat of the jeep, so that she could look directly at him.

"Many many years ago, when I was just ten years old, my mother left home and went away. I haven't seen her since. I know she lives in Calcutta, but we never met after that." Aakash paused, as if trying to recollect. "Anyway, most of my memories of childhood are of my parents' raised voices, arguments, fights, furniture breaking when it was hurled from one end of the room to another. Amongst all this was a tiny, scared boy called Aakash. He didn't know what to do – and so he would run into his room and shut the door and wait for the noises to die down. One day, they died down completely. My mother left without much warning. Maybe it was best for both of them. Maybe my father has been a happier man for the last twenty five years. But the whole affair shattered me. It made me think. And what I decided many years back is still fresh in my mind. I decided that I would never enter into a relationship – because if relationships were so easy to break, then why call them relationships in the first place?"

They had reached Anjali's house. Aakash stopped the jeep with the engine still running. "That's why I decided never to get married," said Aakash. "Now you run along, mix this ingredient with your thought process, and let it alter its path!"

9

Anjali skipped lunch. It was a Sunday and all that had happened through the morning was an active participation by the Sharma household in a debate on Anjali's plan to give her resignation at *Chikitsa* and go back to Safdarjung Hospital. Now, at three in the afternoon, while everyone had dozed off, she moved into her study room, picked up Dr. G. Pickering's book on hypertension and settled down on the sofa to read.

Of course, she couldn't move beyond the page on which she had opened the book. Her mind drifted off to the morning's discussions. She wasn't sure whether Devika was more vociferous about her getting back to *Chikitsa*, or Sunil.

"I went through so much, getting across to Dr Yogi and getting him to put you on his panel of doctors," Devika had said, "And you want to move off to Safdarjung? It doesn't make sense to me at all!"

"Why don't you understand, *bhabi*, I'll be much happier in the work I do at Safdarjung," said Anjali. "My exposure to diseases will be much wider. I'll learn much more."

"You've done MD now – what more do you want to learn?" Devika asked.

Anjali didn't know how to respond to that. With her mouth open, she only gaped at Devika.

Devika yelled out to Bahadur to fetch a glass of water for her and Ajay added to that, saying that he too, wanted one. Sunil got up and switched on the TV and then sat back with the remote in his hand. *Doordarshan* was showing a clip on wild life – a tiger was catching up with a deer which it was chasing. Sunil raised the volume and they all watched, fascinated, as the tiger finally pounced on the deer and brought it down. Then he lowered the volume a bit and turned to Anjali.

"In any case, I don't think there's so much to discuss, Anjali. People nowadays don't get such plush openings so easily. And look at you – you want to give it up and join a government job. If nothing else think of what it will do to your status, at least!"

"A doctor is a doctor, Sunil," Anjali had said. "Where does status come into this?"

"Come off it," said Devika. "That's only in books and movies. In real life doctors only work for the money they rake in!"

"Well, maybe I'm different," Anjali retorted.

She joined back at *Chikitsa* the next morning. She took the car and drove down herself. Dr. Yogi seemed quite pleased to see her. "Welcome back, little lady. You've been out of circulation for two years! Anyway, congratulations for doing so well in your MD exams."

Anjali went down to the reception. Even at ten thirty in the morning, patients were already streaming in. The waiting room was a plush looking hall with murals on the walls and with the ambience that one would find in a good hotel. On the left of the reception was a tall board with the names of the doctors written against each of the specialties available. She glanced up and saw that her name plate was already up against the Medical Specialists – Dr. Anjali Sharma, MBBS, MD. She felt a sense of elation as Prabha, at the reception, looked up and said, "Morning doctor, welcome back. We've allotted a new room to you this time. It's next to Dr. Buhari's on the first floor."

She hadn't been slated with patients in the first half of the day. So she took the time to settle down and set her consultation room the way she wanted. At eleven she buzzed the reception and asked Prabha to get her Dr. Aakash at AIIMS. She gave her the number.

"Hi Aakash —"

"Anju?" said Aakash, not really expecting her call. "You didn't call up yesterday. Have you joined the hospital today?"

"Yes. But Aakash, I'm back at *Chikitsa*, not at Safdarjung."

There was silence at the other end. Anjali could sense that Aakash was upset with her decision.

"Aakash —?"

"Yes, I'm here, Anjali. I think we'll talk later. I've got to rush off right now."

When Anjali put the phone down, she realized that he had called her 'Anjali' after a long time. He must be really upset, she thought.

For the next three days, she wasn't able to contact him. Whenever she would call up, his number would either be engaged or no one would answer the ring.

From the first day itself, the pace of work at *Chikitsa* had picked up so rapidly, that she had no time for herself. She would normally get back home only at about seven in the evening. Every evening, she had been trying Aakash's number, but she just couldn't get to speak to him.

On the fourth day, at the hospital, she got a congratulatory card from Aakash. It had a beautiful picture of a cute little squirrel collecting and accumulating nuts for its house in a tree. There was a terse message in it from Aakash, saying:

Dear Anjali,

Aren't we human beings also like this – rushing out from our cozy dens – only to look at what others are accumulating in life – grabbing what we can – and rushing back to build up our stock in our dens ?

-Aakash

Anjali was angry - angry at him for not even asking or trying to understand what had happened. Her anger lasted till the evening, when she was driving back home. She stopped over at his house and walked into his clinic. A patient was just coming out of his room and the next was getting up to go in with a little baby in her arms. Anjali stole ahead of her.

"If you don't want to talk to me – don't. What are you bugged about, anyway? I told you that I'd do what I want to and just the way I want to. I don't have to justify everything that I do!"

With that, she stormed out of the room, leaving Aakash and his assistant wondering as to the type of hurricane which had just hit the room.

Later in the night, as Aakash lay on his bed before sleeping, his mind drifted off to thoughts of Anjali. He knew he was upset with her decision to go back to *Chikitsa*, but he wasn't sure why. Obviously, she had a right to make up her own mind. It was probably influenced by what her husband and other people of her family guided her into – but then, it had to be. She was living with them. She was related to them and so their desires were bound to have an effect on her thought process. And then it must have been a question of money. Although he had never asked her about it, he guessed the pay at *Chikitsa* must be at least double the pay at a government hospital.

"If that is what has influenced her decision," he thought half aloud, "then it's a very stupid decision." He got up angrily from the bed, put on the light in his room and went out to the balcony.

"But why am I getting upset?" he was doing some soul searching. "She's grown up enough to decide on her own. In fact it's good for her if she can take decisions for herself. For every small little problem in her life, she comes running to me!"

He realized, all at once, that he was fooling himself. There was already a bond between them, and every time she would sit and discuss her problems with him, the bond had been cemented even more. He used to look forward to her calls or to those quick visits to his house sometimes. The excuses were obviously flimsy, but he never heard those excuses.

So why was he upset now? Why did he get upset when Anjali had cancelled the programme to go out with him for lunch? Was it jealously? Was it jealously that her decision to go back to *Chikitsa* was influenced by someone other than himself, and that he hadn't been involved in a decision of hers?

"Don't be stupid," he said to himself. "Why should I be jealous?" Almost simultaneously, he realized once again, that he was hiding feelings from himself. He compressed his lips, angry with himself, as he walked back into his room.

He pulled out the chair and sat at his study table. He switched on the lamp and pulled out a sheet of paper. Many years ago, he had got into the habit of penning his thoughts down in poetry. Most of them were never seen or read by anyone. It was like writing a diary, except that they were never stored with care. At times he would write a poem and then tear it up the next day. Most of the time, however, they would go into a file stored in one of his drawers. He picked up his pen and wrote, almost without pausing.

When you became important to me...
At first all I wanted
was your smile
and then your voice.
I wanted your teasing
and then your laughter.
I wanted your broken omelettes
and then your helplessness.
I wanted affectionate looks
from your lovely eyes
and I wanted the soft hold of your hand.
Now that you have become
so very important to me,
all I want
is you !

When he finished, he read it out to himself. As he put the pen down, he felt as if he was in a whirlpool of thoughts. He, who thought he was always in control of his thoughts, felt them cascading one on top of the other. He had no idea at all of how he was going to control them.

"Have I fallen in love?" he asked himself.

He knew the answer. And he knew that he was walking into a maze. It wasn't as if she was unattached. She was married – and she was 'committed', as she had said. The maze would be endless, and the logical thing was to get out. But when you get into a maze, how do you get out? Which path takes you out and which path takes you deeper in?

Aakash had read somewhere that falling in love was chemistry at work. It was actually a play of chemicals in the brain that gave one the feeling of 'being in love'. And he seemed to be hurtling on without stopping. Wasn't that 'momentum'? Hadn't he studied that in physics at school?

And wasn't it so ironic – a student of biology being entrapped in the mesh of physics and chemistry at eleven o'clock in the night?

The telephone rang. He knew it was Anjali.

Two years went by. Slowly Anjali had got adjusted to the working at *Chikitsa* . She had, in a sense, accepted things as they came along and had started putting in a lot of hard work. She found patients coming in and especially asking to be seen by her. Even Dr. Yogi had, himself, complimented her for her work.

In spite of this, she had a gnawing feeling that she wasn't growing. It was as if she was going through a phase of stagnancy. She was determined not to let it last forever.

And so she started studying genetics. She had been fascinated by the subject for a long time, but had never got down to involving herself in it. Of late, she had been reading a lot about genetics in journals and magazines. She had read about the setting up of the Human Genome Project – an international project funded by six nations. They had plans to identify the half lakh or so genes in human beings and to probably be able to find the manner in which the human DNA was made up. Would it work? Would they really be able to make much progress? And then there was this US based private company called Celera Genomics, headed by Craig Venter, who were simultaneously going into the same secrets of human life. Would their projects be successful? All this fascinated Anjali.

The Centre for Bio-technology at the Jawaharlal Nehru University was quite close to *Chikitsa*, and so whenever she had time, she would go across and pore over journals and books on genetics. She started corresponding with scientists and doctors working in many countries on various projects. Almost all of them would respond – and send her a plethora of research papers which Anjali would read till late at night. All these awakened her to the amount of research being done. At times, she would shut everything and think of how much satisfaction these men and women must be getting through their work. And the next morning, she would be back at *Chikitsa*, prescribing routine medicines for routine illnesses.

She would discuss all this with Aakash and every time he would say, "That's why I keep saying that you are actually cut out for a life in scientific research."

And then both of them would sigh – and leave it at that.

Over those two years, the opportunities that Aakash and Anjali got to meet each other reduced. They spoke a lot on the telephone. Two calls a day to each other seemed to have become a part of their lives. From Greater Kailash, *Chikitsa* was located well beyond AIIMS. So from the time Anjali's MD got over, they had stopped traveling together. Anjali drove to work in one of the Sharmas' Esteems and Aakash continued going to AIIMS in his 'Dinky'.

But they met all the same. Whenever Anjali felt low and down in the dumps, of which the frequency had, of late, become quite a lot, she would ring up Aakash and he would pick her up from outside *Chikitsa*. They would go for a quick lunch either at McDonalds in Vasant Vihar or to some other fast food place. Then there would be

Saturday evenings. It had now become a routine for the Anands and the Sharmas to meet for dinner on almost all Saturday evenings. This routine started when Aakash's father began doing Devika's portrait – a portrait which took its majestic place in the Sharmas' drawing room, overlooking all goings-on in that house, much like the portrait of a queen in a palace! So, although Anjali detested the portrait, she was grateful to it for starting the Saturday evening routine.

Mostly, they met at the Sharmas' house, where Devika would supervise Bahadur's cooking. But once in a while, they would come across to Aakash's house where he and his father would have conjured up a meal of salad, crumb fried chicken, mayonnaise and macaroni – something which Anjali loved.

But Aakash kept complaining about the lack of time with each other. One day at their house, he slipped a piece of paper into Anjali's hand. She quickly closed her hand, hoping that no one had seen the transfer. And then she went to her bathroom to read the short poem.

Excuses , reasons ...
Half lies , half truths ...
Apologies , justifications ...
Manipulations , interpretations ...
Just to be together
for a few moments
stolen
from those who would object ,
from those who wouldn't approve.

But, laws be damned,
those few stolen moments
would make me steal,

again

and again ... !

The next day she spoke to Aakash on the phone. "That was a touchy poem," she said. "Your poems are so nice – why don't you publish them sometime?"

"No," said Aakash. "These are my feelings. I don't share my innermost feelings with anyone – except, maybe with someone who's very important!"

"Aakash, no lunch time meetings this week," said Anjali. "We've got conferences everyday – so I won't know exactly when they'll get over."

"See," complained Aakash. "That's why I crib so much about the lack of time with each other."

"We met just last evening," said Anjali.

"That was with your whole gang around," said Aakash. "I'm talking about 'quality' time."

They laughed.

"In fact, you're so busy, I sometimes wonder if you think of me at all," Aakash complained.

"I don't have a choice," said Anjali in a smug voice. "I have to think of you every day!"

"How come?"

"Your name is the password on my computer!" said Anjali.

It was a normal Monday evening, but what Anjali witnessed that evening left her shaken for many days. It was past six when Anjali finished her rounds of the wards. She came into her room, took off her white coat and picked up her bag to go home.

As she came out of the hospital, she saw a crowd of about twenty five or thirty agitated people, with the hospital staff arguing with them. She stood at the entrance and watched as a couple of people went across to where taxis were parked. One of them obviously was a taxi driver. He drove his taxi up to the gate and as the crowd parted, Anjali saw two people lifting an unconscious man to take him to the taxi. There was blood all over the pavement and the man was still bleeding from his head and from his right arm.

"What's happened?" Anjali asked one of the guards.

He saluted her. "Madam, there was an accident across the road. That man was injured and these people were trying to bring him in here!"

"But why are you sending him off?" Anjali asked.

"Our orders, Madam," said the guard. "Our orders are not to let in such cases. There are all sorts of complications. We told them to go to some other hospital."

"Call them back," Anjali yelled. But by then the taxi had already driven off.

The crowd started dispersing. A few of them stayed behind and walked up to where Anjali was standing. "Are you a doctor here?" asked one of them.

"Yes," said Anjali.

"Aren't you ashamed to call yourself a doctor?" the obviously agitated man was almost yelling. "Aren't you ashamed of this hospital? You people turn away patients who can't pay. What if that man dies? Will none of you even feel guilty?"

The others in the group stopped him and in a while they walked away, leaving a shattered Anjali standing there. Slowly she walked back into the hospital and up to Dr. Buhari's office. He was sitting at his table, studying some case sheets. She went in, sat down and narrated what had happened.

Dr. Buhari merely shrugged. "Oh, you're seeing this kind of thing for the first time. Things like this happen very frequently in Delhi. Dr. Yogi's orders are not to admit such patients. And I agree. They can go to other hospitals. Why should we get into complications of police questioning and all that. And then sometimes nobody turns up to pay the bills. Once, a couple of years back, one accident victim died here after three days. Nobody even came to claim the body, let alone pay the bills!"

Anjali was too shocked to argue. Very woodenly she opened her room and sat there without putting on the lights, her eyes closed. She cried quietly. She knew she'd discuss it with Dr. Yogi the next day. But she cried at the callousness of the system and she cried because she was too small a fry to even make a dent in people's thinking. She cried because she herself had got into a system where the oath of Hippocrates, taken by all doctors was violated so blatantly. She cried because this was not what she had become a doctor for!

And she cried because she hadn't listened to the sane advice that Aakash had given her.

She dialed his number and spoke to him through her tears.

Aakash excused himself from his clinic and took the call in his room. He listened patiently and he let her cry a while. Through her broken sentences, he could only make out an outline of what had happened. He just let her do the talking. He only spoke when he felt that she had let out all the frustration in her.

"Are you feeling any better now?" he asked finally.

"Yes, just talking to you has made me feel lighter," she said.

"Okay – then drive back home," said Aakash. "I'll meet you for a cup of coffee after dinner."

"Aakash—?"

"Yes, Anju?"

"Aakash, I'm sorry," said Anjali. "You were right. I'm not cut out for this kind of life!"

10

In the normal course of things, Devika would have put her foot down even at the suggestion of such an idea. In fact, so would Sunil have. But coming from Aakash, no one really knew how to object.

They were having their dinner when Aakash walked in. "Hi everyone. I'm sorry I'm barging in like this, but I've come with a mission for Anjali."

Bahadur came in with a glass of water for him, while Anjali pushed a bowl of *rosogullas* towards him. They were planning to have *rosogullas* for dessert.

Anjali was curious. "Mission —?"

"I don't know if you'll be agreeable to a thing like this. There's a small village called Chuchundru – it's about 50 km off the main road as you go from Delhi to Meerut. I suppose it's about a hundred kilometers from here. There's been an outbreak of some sort of disease out there. It seems to be taking the form of an epidemic."

"Have there been any deaths?" asked Anjali.

Bahadur was now picking up the plates, as most of them had finished their dinner. He was placing dessert bowls in front of each of them for having their *rosogullas*.

"Yes – I think two of them," said Aakash. "And both were children."

"That's terrible," said Devika, trying to be part of the conversation. "What's being done about it?"

"Well, this village is not too well developed. They've got just one doctor with some sort of makeshift dispensary. He doesn't seem to be able to manage on his own. Yesterday he had come to Delhi to buy a stock of medicines. That's when he asked me to come and help him for ten days or so. He suggested a pediatrician and a medical specialist – and I told him that both are available on this street itself. I've volunteered to go along. How about you, Anjali? Do you think you can get ten days off, for a noble cause?"

"Yes, no problem at all. When, how…, and what else can I ask?"

Ajay's jaw dropped, his mouth open, gaping at the possibility of an explosive reaction from Devika. His hand continued holding the spoon with a piece of rosogulla in it, as if in suspended animation.

Sunil was worried about the administrative arrangements. "How about the stay? Where will Anjali stay?" he asked.

"There are a few well constructed *pucca* houses there. I spoke to the local doctor there - Dr. Harish Bhardwaj. There would be no problem. Anjali would stay with the family of a *zamindar* there and I can pile on with Harish in his quarters."

"How about food?" asked Ajay.

"That's the least of the worries," said Anjali. "Will we drive down from here?"

"Yes, it's a *kutcha* track for about thirty kilometers – but my 'Dinky' should be able to do it."

"Okay. This should be an interesting experience," said Anjali. "Give me tomorrow to tie up things at the hospital and with Dr.Yogi. How about leaving the day after?"

"Fine by me," Aakash said.

"What about Karan?" asked Sunil.

Devika volunteered to help out. "Don't worry. Chanda can look after him in the morning and I'll come back early for the next ten days. Leave Karan to me."

Ajay popped the piece of rosogulla into his open mouth, and went back to savouring the taste, relieved that the explosion he expected from Devika never took place.

Anjali had been to a couple of villages earlier, along with her parents, but on each occasion, it had been for a couple of hours. She had never lived in a village and so she was looking forward to the experience.

Chuchundru turned out to be quite different from what she had expected. They had driven the last thirty kilometers on a dust track. Aakash had fixed up the top hood on the jeep to give them a bit of protection. In spite of that, there were a lot of fine particles of earth settled down all over the interiors of the jeep by the time they reached.

"I wonder how we'll find our way to the dispensary," Aakash thought aloud.

He needn't have worried. By the time they entered the village, news of their arrival had already spread. It was a fairly large village with a population in excess of eight hundred people. Like any other typical village of Uttar Pradesh, there was squalor all around. The lack of hygiene was evident the minute they entered the village. They were guided by the villagers and they drove up to the dispensary, where Dr. Harish was waiting for them. Along with him were the *Pradhan* and five other villagers.

With folded hands, the *Pradhan* and the other villagers expressed their gratefulness. "*Sahib*, it was so nice of you to come to help us. And *Memsahib*'s coming is going to be a blessing to this woe forsaken village. Everything will be alright now!"

The three doctors sat on some rickety chairs pulled out from the dispensary. They quickly got down to work, with Dr. Harish giving them the background of the problem. "It all started about twenty days ago. I had four or five cases of fever and I was treating them like a viral. It's only when one of them died that I started worrying. Now there are more than fifteen men, women and children down with fever. In the last one week another fatality took place."

"Have you observed any commonality of symptoms?" asked Anjali.

"Yes, they all seem to have fever to the order of 102 to 103 degrees. Almost all of them have abdominal discomfort and malaise. Initially, I thought it was Typhoid but since two days back, I've started feeling that it may not be."

"Why did you diagnose Typhoid initially?" asked Aakash.

"Well, as you go around, you'll see that the sanitary conditions are quite appalling. The *Pradhan* has been trying to get the villagers to be more hygienic, but nothing seems to convince them. Where we are now is the affluent part of the village. It's fairly clean here – but as you go towards the fields, you'll see how unhygienic the area is."

They first decided to unload their suitcases and have a wash before going across to the patients. The dispensary had a two room set at its rear, with a small kitchen and a toilet. This was where Dr. Harish was staying. Aakash was to share this with him. Across the street, was the biggest and the best looking house in the village. This belonged to Daya Chand, the *zamindar* and the money lender of the village. Anjali had a separate room given to her there. Aakash went across to see that she was comfortable.

It was well past 3:00 in the afternoon. The three of them had a quick meal prepared by Daya Chand's wife and then they set course to examine the patients.

Anjali asked for the records of each of the patients they saw that afternoon. Dr. Harish would read out from some rough notes that he had. At times, he couldn't even decipher what he had written and most of the time, he used his memory to recall symptoms and the course of treatment he had followed. Anjali glanced at Aakash and found that he was as shocked as she was.

For the whole of the next day, Aakash and Anjali went from house to house examining the patients and making out case sheets for each of them. Most of the patients had very high fever.

"I'm particularly worried about that lady, I think her name is Mayawati," said Anjali, shuffling through the case sheets to find hers. I took her temperature. It was 104 degrees. Her pulse was 105 per minute and she was in a delirium when I was examining her. Her son was the one who died last week." Did you get any stool cultures done, Dr. Harish?" asked Aakash.

"Yes, I did. I had sent three samples to a laboratory in Delhi and I picked up the reports the day I met you. They were all negative for S.Typhi and that's the main reason why I suspect something other than typhoid."

The three doctors sat till late into the night, going through all the records that they had built up through the day – looking for common factors.

"He's been treating all the patients with Chloramphenicol," observed Anjali. "In any case, I think right now we should continue with that."

"I didn't observe any rash on any of the patients," said Aakash. "There's usually a characteristic rash on the upper abdomen which appears in most cases of Typhoid."

Anjali looked up from her notes. "Yes, but that's not too indicative. In Typhoid, the small lesions which you're talking about, are mostly observed in the second week of the illness. So maybe it'll show up in the patients in a few days."

Anjali yawned and stretched herself. She was sleepy and in any case, it was past ten in the night. Villagers usually go to bed early, she thought. Then, she wasn't sure of the reaction of her hosts if she stayed out too late. People staying in villages are fairly conservative in nature as compared to those staying in cities. So, although she generally would not have bothered, she thought it best to go back to her room in Daya Chand's house.

She slept soundly and wouldn't have woken up if it wasn't for the persistent pounding on the door of her room by Daya Chand's daughter, Nimmo. She strutted in with a cup of tea for Anjali.

"*Doctorni Sahib*, if I hadn't woken you up, you would have slept till lunch time," Nimmo chattered away. "Do all people from the cities sleep till so late? Anyway, we've already had breakfast and *Doctor Sahib* at the dispensary has been asking about you."

Anjali looked at her watch. It was past seven. She jumped out of bed. "Oh my gosh," she yelled, cutting short Nimmo's chatter. "I was supposed to be at the dispensary at six thirty."

She rushed through her bath, changed her clothes and rushed out to the dispensary. Aakash and Harish had already left for their rounds, leaving Harish's assistant to bring her to them. She caught up with them at Mayawati's house.

"Hi, good morning," Aakash smiled at her. "You've got some catching up to do.

"I don't know where you get so much energy from. Don't you ever get tired?" Anjali mumbled under her breath so that she wasn't audible to him. Then she got straight down to work. "How's she?"

"Well, you'll be glad to know that her fever has dropped considerably. It's just 99 degrees right now," said Harish.

Mayawati's husband was by her side. "The fever was quite high till late in the night, then she perspired a lot and in the morning when I felt her forehead, it wasn't so hot. But when I tried to give her some milk, she vomited."

After examining her, they went around to the other patients. Although Anjali had reservations about the caliber of Harish as a doctor, she was impressed by the fact that he and the *Pradhan* had organized things quite efficiently. A group of ten men and women volunteers had got together and they were doing things as Harish had directed.

Three houses away, a boy of about eighteen was on the bed for the last two days. "Just three days back, he was working in the fields," his mother lamented. "He was perfectly okay. When he came back, he said he was feeling cold. I just laughed at him and I told him that he must be mad – it was so warm around here. But he kept saying that he was cold, so I pulled down a blanket for him. An hour later he got up to go to the toilet. He was walking as if he was drunk. I got suspicious and so I went and smelt him. But no – all he smelt of was onions, which he had along with his *rotis* for lunch. And then he vomited and fell down. Since then he's been on the bed. Sometimes, he doesn't even recognize us. I've been putting a wet cloth on his forehead every now and then but his skin feels as if it's burning!"

"Don't worry, *maiji*," Anjali consoled her. "He'll be alright."

While Aakash was examining him, Anjali went through his case sheet. "He's on Chloramphenicol," she said. "He's reported constipation and headaches for the last two days."

The house next door had a man of thirty, prostrate on the bed with fairly similar symptoms. Again, the illness had started with chills and went on to high fever. The man was able to talk and he went through his symptoms all over again. "On the first day, I had a lot of pain in my stomach, but that's reduced."

"Do you drink?" asked Aakash, examining his abdomen.

"Occasionally, *sahib*. But not very much," he said.

For a while Aakash looked curiously at a small red spot close to his navel. It was a small papule, but it looked as if it might enlarge and as if it was filling with pus.

Aakash turned to Anjali when he finished examining the patient. "No enlargement of the liver or spleen," he said. "They're not palpable."

They went through the examinations with six more patients. Then while going back, at lunch time, Anjali decided to stop for a while at Mayawati's house. Her husband was sitting on the floor as Mayawati slept. Anjali opened her bag and took out a thermometer. There was a deathly silence in the house as she waited for the instrument to register. A minute later, when she took it out, it showed a temperature of below 98 degrees. She put it back again, but even a minute later, it remained at the same level. Mayawati kept sleeping.

As she walked back to the dispensary, Anjali was wondering. She should have been glad at the fever having gone, but the pallor on the lady's face scared her. Through many cases in the last few years, she felt she had an intuition when things were going wrong. She had a similar feeling now. She carried on walking woodenly to the dispensary, a foreboding of death on her mind.

It was around four in the evening when one of the women volunteers came running to the dispensary, where the three of them were comparing notes. "*Doctorni sahib*, Mayawati's condition has become bad again. She's jabbering nonsense and her skin has become very hot again."

All three of them went to Mayawati's house. Her husband was sitting on the floor exactly in the same position, not sure at all of what he should be doing. Mayawati's temperature had shot up to 105 degrees. A sudden thought made Anjali ask all the men to go out. "I want to examine her inguinal area," she said.

Only the woman helper and Anjali stayed inside. Aakash and Harish stood outside, looking out towards the fields. A few buffaloes were coming back in a herd after spending the day grazing. The small boy who was herding them together came running to Harish when he saw him. Harish picked him up and rummaged in his pockets to finally pull out a hard boiled sweet which the boy gleefully grabbed out of his hand. Then he got down and ran away as quickly as he came. Not a word had been exchanged between them.

When Anjali came out, she was ashen faced. One look at her and Aakash realized that something serious was the matter.

"Anjali…?"

"The lady's dying," the words came out of Anjali's mouth with difficulty. "I don't think there's very much we can do."

"And…," asked Aakash, knowing that there was more to come.

Anjali led the way and Aakash and Harish followed, as she walked rapidly towards the dispensary. She looked as if she had seen a ghost.

"Aakash," she said finally. "You have to go back tomorrow. You go back to Delhi. I'll be here for some time."

"Don't be so stupid, Anju," said Aakash. "What is it?"

"Aakash, it's Plague!" said Anjali as she slumped into a chair.

"Oh my good God," said a shocked Aakash. "You mean you could see a bubo?"

"Two of them," said Anjali. "Two buboes in her femoral region!"

For a while the three doctors sat in the dispensary, each of them lost in thought. Bubonic Plague! So much had been written and so much had been talked about this disease. It was so well known and feared in the olden ages. So many famous authors had written about it. Aakash's mind went to what he had read about Plague – the pandemics in the fourteenth century and in China in the nineteenth century. He thought of the fear and deaths it had caused in its wake. Now almost the whole world thought it was a disease of the past. And here it was – staring at them in the face!

The buboes which Anjali had seen are the characteristic indication of bubonic plague. The human body has, besides blood vessels, an independent system of vessels constituting the lymph system. This system carries lymph – a clear, colourless fluid resembling blood. In bubonic plague, regional lymph nodes get inflamed and enlarged because of an abnormal accumulation of fluid in the intercellular spaces of the body. These, then, show up as buboes.

Barely an hour later the *Pradhan* came and called Harish aside to tell him that Mayawati had died. Aakash and Anjali stayed behind, while Harish went to her house. As soon as he left, Anjali looked imploringly at Aakash. "Go back, Aakash. Please go back. If something were to happen to you, I wouldn't know what to do."

"Nothing will happen to any of us, Anju," said Aakash, holding her hand and looking directly at her moist eyes. "We've come here together – we'll do something for this village – we'll make them smile again – and then we'll go back together. Now before you burst into tears, let's do some planning."

"Yes," said Anjali. "I think the first thing we need to do is to isolate the patients."

Aakash smiled and nodded his head. He always marveled at Anjali's ability to jump from melancholy to spirited action. He knew that a few moments later, she'd be back at organizing things.

Anjali frowned as she looked at Aakash. It was uncanny how, of late, both of them had been able to read each other's thoughts.

"Sinusoidal wave ... ?" she asked. That's how Aakash used to tease her for her mood swings. He nodded. Then he focused his thoughts back to the present.

When Harish came back, he slipped in quietly into the vacant chair. "I haven't told anyone as yet of what we think it is. Don't you think we should tell the *Pradhan*?"

"Yes," said Aakash. "I think we should call him and let him be with us as we organize things now onwards."

"They're planning to cremate Mayawati's body right away," Harish announced. "They've started the arrangements already."

"Anju, do you think an autopsy would serve any purpose?" asked Aakash." Do you think we should send the body for a post-mortem?"

"No, I don't think so," Anjali was thoughtful. "There'll be too many hazards in that. But we need to take a blood sample and I'll go myself and aspirate some interstitial fluid from the centre of one of her buboes. Then, if lab checks confirm the presence of Y.pestis, we'd know for sure."

What she was talking about was Yersinia pestis, the bacteria which is known to be the causative agent of plague. Primarily, plague is a disease of rodents. Rats are a known reservoir and they always act as a source for human infection. Diseased rats suffer from and die from plague. Sometimes it appears as a chronic form in the rodents and this keeps the infection smoldering. The rat fleas become infected after having a blood meal from a rat. But once the rat dies, they don't like to stick on to its cooling body. So they leave their host and find the warm body of another rat, only to infect the second rat and thus starting a cycle which carries on. Sometimes, the fleas transmit the disease from the rodents to human beings after having fed on the blood of an infected rat.

Aakash and Harish accompanied Anjali back to Mayawati's house. This time Anjali wore rubber gloves as she syringed samples of blood from the body. Then she punctured one of the buboes and syringed a sample of the fluid. Carefully, she put the bottles into a small box and then sealed it with adhesive plaster.

Back in the dispensary, Aakash suggested that either he or Harish should drive up to Meerut in the night itself so that the lab checks could be done first thing in the morning.

"I'll go," said Harish. "I, too, have a jeep. I bought it so that I had a vehicle which could negotiate the *kutcha* roads easily."

Before Harish could go, the three doctors had a lot of work to do. The first thing they decided to do was to isolate the patients. This was important, but they had to wait for the *Pradhan* to come back from the funeral to discuss how they would go about doing the isolation and which place could be used as a makeshift hospital.

"This epidemic is still in the budding stage," said Anjali. "We've got to nip it right here, before it gets into the pneumonic stage.

What she meant was that plague, in the bubonic form, rarely results in transmission from man to man. It occurs only through bites from fleas which have fed on the blood of an infected rat. The blood of an infected human being will rarely have enough bacteria for the disease to be transmitted to another human. But the dangerous part is that if the treatment doesn't begin soon enough, lesions develop in the lungs of some of the patients and then plague takes the form of pneumonia. This is the starting point for a human being-to-human being transmission of airborne pneumonic plague, which is difficult to control.

Then there was the question of treatment. "We need large amounts of Streptomycin and Tetracycline injections," said Anjali. "Although Harish's administration of Chloramphenicol has probably restricted the epidemic, we need to change over now to Streptomycin and Tetracycline."

Taking the lead from Anjali, Aakash and Harish got down to

calculating the amount of medicine that Harish would have to buy.

"We'll also need Konamycin for some patients if their resistance to Streptomycin increases," said Anjali.

When they finished with medicines, syringes, dressings, antiseptics and the other items they needed for the patients – and for other likely patients – they had a long list running into five handwritten pages.

"You go to a Dr AK Mishra – he's one of the deans at Meerut Medical College," said Aakash. "I'll ring him up from here. Wake him up at whatever time you reach, so that by early morning the tests are started. Then, you start collecting our supplies."

"What about the money angle?" asked Anjali.

"I'll tell AK. He'll tie up things on credit right now," Aakash replied. "Then we can think of how we'll sort it out."

Next, they got down to making lists of what they needed to control the disease. "We'll have to first attack the fleas," said Aakash. "So we'll need about two tons of DDT. Then we'll need other insecticides – probably Aldrin or Dieldrin."

When their lists were complete, they did a rough calculation and realized that they would need about two lakh Rupees. None of them had any clue as to where the money would come from.

"If I go through official channels, or to the ministry, it'll take at least ten to fifteen days to get the medicines or other supplies," said Harish.

"I know an NGO which would be willing to help," Aakash remembered the organization which went about doing charitable work in Delhi. "I'll try and contact them on the phone."

"And I'll give a call to Dr. Yogi," said Anjali. "*Chikitsa* should be able to contribute. I'll ask him to send across at least fifty thousand rupees."

"You think that set-up would?" Aakash was skeptical. He turned towards Harish. "Anyway, for our immediate needs, Dr. Mishra would tie up things, I'm sure."

"Try and get some help too, if you can," suggested Anjali. "A couple of doctors and about ten nurses would be a big help."

By the time Harish could drive away, it was past ten in the night. In the meanwhile, the *Pradhan* discussed with Daya Chand and a few other villagers as to where they could set up a make-shift hospital.

The entire village stayed up that night. The news of the suspicion of the doctors that it might be plague, had spread like wildfire. Almost all the villagers first congregated in a big open space in the centre of the village. Aakash had already spoken to the *Pradhan* and to Daya Chand. Both wielded a tremendous amount of power in the village – one because of the position he was in and the other because of the money that he had. Either way, both Aakash and Anjali thought it best to let the two of them handle the rest of the villagers. The two doctors had first sat and explained the seriousness of the situation and then had told them what they would have to emphasize to the villagers.

"The most important and urgent task is to isolate all the patients," Anjali told the *Pradhan*. "There's no hospital here, so we'll have to set up one in a couple of houses – where we can put about thirty beds. That way only a few of us would be exposed to the patients."

"You will have to talk to the villagers and then organize this," Aakash continued. "Also of paramount importance is that not a single person from this village goes out till this epidemic is over. You will have to explain that this would be best for them and for the rest of the country. We'll fight this epidemic here itself and you watch, we'll win very soon."

Luckily, the *Pradhan* was a very tough man who everyone had a lot of respect for. In no uncertain terms, he made it clear that for the next few weeks there was to be no talk of caste differences. All the patients would be housed together and would be treated together. A few feeble protests by some of the upper caste villagers were quickly put down. In any case, they realized by themselves that with the meager resources in the village, there could be no alternative.

"Not one of you is to step out of this village," the Pradhan boomed. He went on to explain the reasons and then added a threat. "If you do go out, for whatever reason, you will not be allowed to come back to this village once this problem is over. And by the grace of *Bhagwan*, we will get over with this crisis in just a few days!"

Mayawati's husband volunteered to let his house be used. It was large and spacious. Then with a bit of coaxing, the two houses on either side were also vacated by their owners. By two in the morning, beds were arranged in the three houses. The group of volunteers, which had been helping the doctors, then used a couple of beds as stretchers and shifted the patients into the 'wards', as Aakash started calling them. By six in the morning, the patients, numbering twenty eight, had been moved.

By early morning too, Anjali and Aakash realized that the condition of almost half the patients was now serious. In the last twenty four hours, buboes had grown in quite a few of them – some in the groin, some under the arms. Two of them were keeping their heads sideways to relieve the discomfort from the swelling in their necks.

As they went around making the patients comfortable, Anjali was getting more and more worried. "We need medicines quickly now, Aakash. See this little girl – her name is Payal – she's had some hemorrhage. You can see this area of necrosis." Anjali showed Aakash small areas of dead tissue which had turned black.

"Chin up, Anju," said Aakash. "By evening we'll be fully operational.

Harish's arrival back in the evening was heralded with such fanfare, that he forgot his tiredness all at once. Along with his jeep came two trucks – one filled to the top with DDT – and another carrying cases of medicines, equipment and also the insecticides which Aakash had ordered. The trucks stopped about a half kilometer outside Chuchundru, offloaded their wares in double quick time and then headed back with their drivers not uttering a word, lest some germs enter their mouths.

Harish hadn't managed any doctors, but had brought along two volunteer nurses. "And meet Mr. Sushant Kumar," he introduced. He's a freelance journalist. He had come to meet Dr Mishra and he smells a story here – so he's going to spend a few days with us."

As another group of villagers organized the shifting of the DDT onto bullock carts, Harish talked about what he had done in Meerut. "The reports on the lab checks were going to take time so I left. They said we'd get the results by evening. Aakash, you'll have to give a call to Dr Mishra. Otherwise, I've managed to get almost everything that we listed."

Aakash went off to give a call to Meerut. Dr Mishra had all the details ready for him. The laboratory had done staining of the specimen with fluorescent specific antiserum and had confirmed the presence of Y. pestis. Large numbers of morphologically characteristic bacilli were seen in the stained smear of the fluid from the bubo.

As Aakash read back the reports to Anjali from the paper on which he had noted down the results, she nodded grimly. "Well, that confirms things," she said. "What about the blood cell count?"

"WBC was 25000 cells per cc. With a predominance of polymorphonuclear leukocytes," said Aakash. "RBC was normal."

Everything confirmed bubonic plague!

Chuchundru remained awake through the night once again. Anjali and the nurses looked after the in-patients, administering Streptomycin injections to them every four hours. "We'll give this for forty eight hours and then we'll decrease the dose to six hourly after that," Anjali guided the nurses.

Aakash and Harish formed teams with the list of names of all the villagers. They started giving them Sulfadiazine tablets. "It'll act well for prevention of the spread of the disease," Anjali had told them. "There are some vaccines available in America, but I don't think they are available in India. In any case, Sulfa will help."

Simultaneously, another group got together along with the insecticides and went around the houses spraying them and disinfecting them. The previous day, Aakash had stopped the villagers from using rat poison. "Don't kill the rats," he had explained to them. "The fleas which spread the disease prefer the rodents to human beings. It's only when rats die, do they move on to humans. So we'll have to be liberal with insecticide and try and eliminate fleas first. Then we'll kill the rats."

For the next two weeks, only the doctors, the nurses and the group of ten volunteers were allowed to come near the patients. An exception was made in the case of Sushant, the journalist, who came to spend a day or two, but stayed on to help. But all of them were administered tetracycline regularly as a preventive treatment.

It was on the seventh day that Anjali broke out with fever. Early in the morning she woke up with pains in her muscles and a splitting headache. At first she thought an Aspirin and a cup of tea would do the trick. But when she took her own temperature and read off 103 degrees on the thermometer, she collapsed back onto the bed and asked Nimmo to call Aakash.

Very quickly, she was shifted into one of the rooms in the dispensary, which wasn't being used now in any case. Immediately Aakash started her off on intravenous injections of tetracycline. For almost the whole of that day, he sat next to her, using cold swabs on her forehead and taking her temperature every hour. He was a very worried man.

Anjali slept for most of the time. She smiled at him once when she woke up. "Don't be so worried, Aakash," she said. "Nothing will happen to me."

She reached out for him, and he held her hand in his, tightly. For a while, a surge of affection for her, replaced the worry that was in his mind. He bent down and kissed her forehead.

"Go back to sleep, Anju," he said softly. And she did, almost immediately.

In the afternoon, one of the women volunteers sat with her, as Aakash went back to the patients. In the last five days, quite a dramatic turnaround had taken place. After Mayawati, a young boy of about seventeen had died. But since then, the disease seemed to be under control. The number of people who were obviously affected by the plague had gone up to thirty five within the first two days but then it remained at that figure.

The village itself had undergone a sea change. Gone were the dirty & clogged sewers, piles of garbage and pools of stagnant water. Even before the arrival of the members of *Sahayata*, the organization in Delhi which Aakash had approached, the villagers themselves had started the cleanup operation. Insecticides had been sprayed in all the houses and on stagnant water. The fumigation must have had its effect because for the last three days, no new cases had been reported. In fact, barring Anjali, no reports of even mild fever had come in.

Sahayata came in with money, food, tents, relief material and above all the twenty eager men, ready to put in their best and expecting nothing in return. Just one phone call from Aakash on the second day had made this possible.

The day after Dr. Harish had returned from Meerut, Anjali had made a call to Dr. Yogi and ask for monetary help from *Chikitsa*. First of all Dr. Yogi had been very skeptical of their diagnosis.

"It can't be plague, little lady," he said with finality. "India has officially declared eradication of plague as long back as 1966!" But then he had listened while Anjali described the symptoms and then the laboratory reports which had confirmed the presence of Y. pestis.

Anjali went on to describe what was happening at the village and when she told him about the presence of the journalist, Dr. Yogi suddenly changed his attitude. "Actually, it wouldn't be a bad idea, he said. "You must make sure he reports our contribution. Give him a little brief of my background and what I have been doing and that you're from this hospital. We'll be able to get some mileage out of this if his reports get published."

Anjali had made it appear as if there was some disturbance in the line. And then she had disconnected the line and had not called up again.

It had become dark when Aakash suddenly saw the woman volunteer who he had left with Anjali. She was back in the 'wards', helping the patients.

"What are you doing here?" he asked angrily. "You were supposed to be looking after the *Doctorni*."

"She sent me off," said the lady. "Her fever has come down and she said she would be coming here after some time."

A stab of fear went through Aakash. He remembered Mayawati's case. He knew also, that the course of bubonic plague is marked by irregular fever, and that a sudden drop to sub normal is a warning sign of the progress of the disease.

He left what he was doing and went rushing to the dispensary. Anjali wasn't on the bed. But before he could even get angry, she walked in - with her wet hair open. She had gone across to Daya Chand's house for a bath.

"Anju, how can you have a bath in this condition?" asked Aakash. "You know it's incorrect. Just get straight back into bed."

"Relax, Aakash," said Anjali. "Here, feel my forehead." She came across, close to him. "See, there's no temperature. I think it was just exhaustion. We haven't slept very much for so many days. The lack of sleep must have caught up with me."

Suddenly Aakash was relieved and with that, he realized that he too, was exhausted. He hadn't slept for more than a couple of hours every night for the last one week. He slumped down on Anjali's bed and felt as if the energy had drained out of him.

Anjali came and sat next to him and continued combing her hair. "I know you were very worried Aakash, but I was sure I hadn't caught the plague. I just needed sleep. And before you fall ill, you go and have a good night's rest today while I look after things."

Through his tiredness, he looked at Anjali and saw her as a very beautiful woman. As she ran the comb through her hair, a wave of desire went through him. His hands wanted to reach out and touch her, but he closed his eyes instead.

In the darkness that engulfed him, the fresh fragrance of Anjali's skin and hair reached him. He took a deep breath, as if he were a drowning man, gasping for breath, taking one last breath before he went down again.

All at once he felt her moist lips on his forehead and then all his resistance broke down. He reached out for her, put his hand behind her head and drew her close to him. But she pulled away.

His eyes were still closed and he felt defeated. He didn't want to open his eyes again. He didn't want to see the scorn on her face.

"Wait," he heard her say. Then he heard her close the latch of the door.

When her lips touched his, it was just for a fleeting moment at first. He opened his eyes and looked at her, at the deepness of her light brown eyes, at the hint of a smile on her mouth. He felt her fragrance going deep inside him and the touch of her hair as it cascaded around his head. He reached out once again.

They kissed as if they had been denying themselves this for a very long time. He felt the softness of her lips as his tongue parted them and went in to explore, finding her tongue and probing as if both were clashing for a right of way.

When they broke apart, he stroked her face gently, running a finger over her nose and her lips. This time, her eyes were shut tight. "You know what," said Aakash, "your kiss tastes like a green apple - delicious and succulent!"

She laughed. "Haven't you heard?" she said, "An apple a day keeps the doctor away!"

"Yes, "said Aakash "But nobody figured out what happens when you have two in a day!"

And he reached out for her again.

11

The "Times of India" carried Sushant Kumar's report on the front page. Datelined 23rd April 1999, it brought out the story from the beginning.

"These three doctors were the messiahs of this hitherto unknown village. The village, Chuchundru, now owes its existence to them. In fact, the whole nation is proud of them for the method in which this mini-epidemic was handled." Anjali was reading out from a copy of the newspaper as Aakash drove back towards Delhi.

The doctors had refused to give the reporter their photographs, but somehow he had sneaked in one picture of all three of them outside their make shift hospital.

Anjali continued reading. "Most people would have run away from possible death. Not only did these three brave the disease themselves, they managed to rally around the people of the entire village, as if they were some sort of leaders.

Albeit unwillingly, suddenly they had become heroes. Aakash knew that it wouldn't make a difference to him. He would just get back to his clinic and things would settle down pretty soon. Anjali on the other hand was sure that there would be a good amount of hullaballoo at *Chikitsa*. She didn't know how she was going to handle that. In fact, she grimaced as she thought of even the reaction in her family. Both Sunil and Devika would start by having their friends over and then there would be numerous parties, where she would have to keep explaining the whole story to people who wouldn't understand.

They drove on silently for a while - both reminiscing about the events of the last two weeks. It was exactly fourteen days since they had driven into Chuchundru. Now they were driving back after being sure that there were no traces of plague left in the village.

Anjali turned to Aakash. "You know, I have a lot to thank you for," she told him. "In these two weeks, I think I've done so much that I'm going back a very satisfied person."

"For me, the scene this morning, as we left, said it all," Aakash mused.

It had been a poignant scene. The whole village was there to see them off. The village, which was in gloom just a fortnight back, was suddenly full of life. All the villagers wanted to touch the feet of the doctors in reverence, something which both of them had a difficult time avoiding. Aakash was dead against this whole custom and he had made it clear to the villagers - but at that moment no one cared about what he felt. After all, did they bother about whether their deities enjoyed being bathed in milk? They did it anyway.

Aakash and Anjali had to promise, at least a hundred times, that they would not forget the people of Chuchundru and that they would visit them whenever they could. It took almost an hour for them to say their goodbyes and for them to be able to extract themselves from all the villagers milling around them. The only time when everyone went silent for a while, was when Aakash and Anjali cut through the crowd and went to the back, where Mayavati's husband stood quietly to one side, away from the rest of the crowd. He had lost both his son and his wife in these two weeks, and for him, the story of Chuchundru's plague had ended when Mayawati had died. For a while he stared vacantly into space, as Aakash stood close to him. Then, all of a sudden, he put his head on Aakash's chest and cried like a small child.

"Cup of tea?" asked Aakash as they drew close to a *Dhaba*.

"No, but I wouldn't mind a Thums-Up, "said Anjali".

It was very odd weather for the month of April. Normally it should have been hot. But it had been cloudy since early morning. Now, thick black clouds had gathered and it seemed as if it would rain.

The little boys at the *Dhaba* came running out and quickly started laying out a table and two chairs. But Aakash brushed them aside and went to the *charpoys*. He knew Anjali would prefer to sit on them.

They sat quietly for a long time, well after their Thums-Up got over, gazing at the clouds - thick black clouds rushing by, chasing each other, mingling with each other and becoming more and more ominous. The sky was almost totally overcast and even at noon, it felt as if it was late evening.

Suddenly out of a small break in the clouds, a beam of sunlight came through. It was like a narrow path between the ground and the sky. Both of them looked at it in fascination.

"Wow, it looks so lovely," said Anjali, totally enthralled.

"Coming for a walk on it?" Aakash teased her.

"Where will it lead us?"

"I don't know," said Aakash, "What I do feel is that if you choose a path and stay on it, it has to lead you to a good destination."

"But if you were given a choice, what would you choose as a destination?"

Again Aakash laughed. "That's easy. Any destination where there's happiness along the path".

"Like what you did in the last two weeks?"

"Yes that - and where you could be with me alongside."

"Does that really mean all that much to you - me being alongside?" asked Anjali.

"Let's see if this answers your question," said Aakash, pulling out a piece of folded paper from his shirt pocket. "I wrote this last night while I was packing my stuff."

Sitting on the charpoy, Anjali read out the poetry of Aakash's feelings.

I once had a very good friend.
She was with me constantly.
She was dark -
but I got used to it.
She was quiet -
but I would talk to her.
I could never be scared of anything !
Every time I had a problem
I would run to her arms.
She would embrace me
and I would be lost in her for hours .
*Her name was - **Loneliness** .*

Then like Sunrise , you came along...
The darkness melted and I found joy in everything.
The trees were greener , the skies were bluer ,
there was so much to talk about,

so much to laugh about.
You made me feel important,
you made me feel good.
You made it possible to feel - deeply,
to enjoy freely , to be needed.

But now I am scared...
I am scared of not getting your time.
I am scared of being unimportant.
I am scared of - Sunset !
Because if I ever lose you,
with what face
will I go back
to Loneliness ?

At the end of it, she took a deep breath, and read it all over again, to herself this time. Then she folded the sheet of paper and put it in her bag.

"Why did you write this, Aakash?" she asked. "Do you really think you won't get my time. How can you think of ever being unimportant to me?"

"Anju, you are married," said Aakash. "And remember - you spoke of the 'commitment' that you had!"

"Yes, but that was centuries ago - hasn't so much water flowed under the bridge since then?

It didn't seem strange to either of them that even for the rest of the journey back, they only kept recalling events of the last fourteen days - as if they knew deep inside that the togetherness that they had shared would soon come to an end - as if they were trying to cling-on to the events of that fortnight, in the hope that they could prolong the time before they had to get back to their routines.

Anjali kept recalling the way all the villagers had rallied together. "I think it was just lucky that every one acted like one big family," she said.

Aakash talked of the way the funds for the supplies had got sorted out. *Sahayata* had pitched in with the initial contribution. And then, on the day that Anjali was in bed with fever, two representatives of the Ministry of Health had visited the village. Dr. Mishra's clout in the medical circles and the presence of a journalist at the scene acted as catalyst to their decision. They took on the onus of clearing the bills and that took the worry off the heads of the three doctors at *Chuchundru*. In any case, till then they hadn't really had the time to worry about how Dr. Mishra was going to clear all the bills.

After Nizamuddin bridge, for the remaining twenty minutes or so to Greater Kailash, Aakash drove his 'Dinky' with only his right hand. He even did some acrobatic manoeuvres of changing gears with his right hand, reaching across the steering to the gear lever. Anyone watching from outside would have thought that his left arm had been incapacitated.

It had been - in a sense. His left hand was holding Anjali's hand, fingers entwined, neither of them willing to let go.

Five fingers
- touching another five.
Five fingers
- entwined in each other.

Five fingers
- causing sparks to fly.
Five fingers
Sometimes caressing,
Sometimes cajoling,
Sometimes exploring,
Sometimes discovering.
Sometimes just quiet, holding on to the other five.
Quiet in the thought
That together,
- they could have made,
a formidable ten !

Finally they reached. Aakash got off and went across to her side, to help Anjali out of the jeep. "Here you are, ma'am," he said. All safe and sound as promised – back to your home."

Anjali didn't get off.

"Let me tell you one thing, if you haven't already understood," she said. "This is my house – this is where I stay. Home is where I live – where my heart and soul live. And I do hope you know where that is!"

With that, she picked up her suitcase from the rear of the jeep and marched up to her house.

12

Devika, herself, had chosen all the gifts. And now they were spread on the dining table with Sunil and Ajay examining them before they were certified fit. Although giving gifts was quite a routine thing in their business, these gifts were for a purpose.

A new sales tax officer had been posted to the Kashmere Gate area. Unlike the earlier one who wouldn't bother to check the sales tax returns, this officer was young and enthusiastic. In his agenda was a plan to make sure that the business-*wallahs* didn't cheat the government of the sales tax which should be paid.

For years, small business establishments never bothered about sales tax. The modus operandi was simple. No bills were given to customers. Almost all transactions took place on slips of paper with no record thereafter.

This suited both the customer and the seller. Of course, a few transactions took place on proper bills so as to establish some semblance of order in an otherwise chaotic system.

The old shopkeepers of Kashmere Gate had told Devika not to worry.

"It's only the initial enthusiasm that the officer will have," they told her. "In a few weeks, he'll get used to the system and will move with it. There'll be a fixed quota for his pockets and you'll see, there are very few people who don't have big pockets."

When Anjali came back after her day at *Chikitsa*, she was summoned into the drawing room before she had a chance to even pick up Karan.

"What's all this?" she asked.

As Sunil did the explaining, she nodded absently. The gifts looked lovely – a twenty piece crystal bar set for the officer, a saree for his wife and expensive electronic games for his children. But, Anjali was too tired to really appreciate them.

She was looking forward to a quiet Saturday evening, the next day, with probably a visit by Aakash thrown in as a bonus. So, when Sunil said, "*Bhabi* wants the two of us to go tomorrow and give the gifts," she again, just nodded.

It was later in the night, when she was chatting with Aakash on the phone, that she realized the crassness of the whole situation.

"It's funny how we all crib about the magnitude of corruption in India," said Aakash. "And then, in some way or the other, we all contribute to it."

"What do you suppose I should do?" asked Anjali.

"Drill some sense into them all. Why can't they just pay all the taxes, rather than going about bribing some sales tax inspector?" suggested Aakash.

"I'm sure they won't understand," said Anjali.

The next morning when Anjali brought up the topic, expectedly Devika was the one who carried forth the discussion.

"This is not a bribe, Anjali, it's just a gift."

"Oh, what's the difference – we're giving it with the same motive," said Anjali.

Sunil retorted to that. "A bribe would have to be much bigger, lots of cash and all that. These are just small tokens of friendship."

"But the aim is the same, isn't it," asked Anjali, "that he turns a blind eye at our not paying the due taxes?"

"We're not the only ones; everyone is doing the same," said Sunil.

"That's no reason, Sunil. If others are doing something wrong, it doesn't justify our doing the same," said Anjali.

The argument went on and on, with Ajay joining in, and with voices being raised to the 'normal' high-decibel levels, which were so common to even usual conversations in the Sharma household. Anjali, as always, felt cornered, but was in no mood to give up her attempt at trying to convince the others.

The discussion ended abruptly when Sunil got up and went into the bedroom saying with finality – "there's no sense in trying to convince you, Anjali. You just won't understand these things."

That evening, Anjali went along with Sunil to the sales-tax inspector's house to give the gifts to him. It wasn't as if she was convinced that it was right, it was just that she didn't want to make an issue out of something which she was sure she wouldn't be able to convince the rest of the family about. Added to it was the fact that she didn't have the energy, or the inclination to fight with them, even though her views remained exactly the same.

"You know, Aakash, I've developed this uncanny ability of being able to put up a front which is so different from what I feel from within," she told Aakash when they spoke about it later that evening. "The other guy just isn't able to make out that I have an opinion bang opposite to what I'm talking about to him."

"You mean you turned on your charm at that sales tax inspector?" Aakash was astonished.

"The poor guy didn't have a chance. He was convinced that I was a simple, *seedha-sadha*, business-man's wife, and that we were just trying to be on the right side of the wrong guy!"

"God, Anju! That leaves me with lots of questions in my mind. How much of what you say to me, should I trust?" asked Aakash.

"Oh, shut up, will you," said Anjali. "Anyway, aren't you annoyed at me for agreeing to go with Sunil on this stupid exercise?"

"No," said Aakash. "I guess I understand that bit you said about 'commitment'. And as part of married life, you will have to go along with what he wants to do."

"That's crap, and you know it. And don't keep harping on that 'commitment' bit, just because I happened to say it once," said Anjali. "I also happened to have told you that lots of things have happened since then."

The bedroom door flew open as Sunil and Devika barged into the room. They were discussing how misbehaved the neighbour's children were, and how they just wouldn't listen to what Devika would tell them.

Seeing her on the phone, Sunil asked "Who are you talking to?"

"Oh, just another doctor," said Anjali.

"The truth, but not the whole truth!" she continued into the mouthpiece to Aakash, as she walked out of the room with the cordless telephone in her hand.

13

Anjali got pushed into the world of genetics just by chance. If it wasn't for the two movies she saw, and the book she read, she might have continued with her job at *Chikitsa*. Ironically, it was Yogi who gave her the two video cassettes. He had a penchant for science-fiction movies and he would pick up cassettes of movies whenever he would travel abroad. Anjali was glancing through his collection, waiting for him in his cabin one day, when he came in.

"Have a look at these two," he said, pulling out two video cassettes from the shelf on the side wall. "Although the movies were made about fifteen years ago, they were really futuristic in their thought process."

Anjali got around to seeing the first one on a quiet Sunday afternoon, when everyone in the house went off for their ritual holiday siesta. Karan came in excitedly when he saw her putting the cassette into the VCR and he sat with her through the movie.

"Sleeper" was a Woody Allen film, in which he himself has starred, with Diana Keaton opposite him. It was the plot which intrigued Anjali. The movie was about a jazz musician in Manhattan, who is cryogenically frozen against his will. And then he is kept in that state and revived only two hundred years later. He is then in an advanced society, where he is the only one without a biometric identity.

"Is it possible?" she asked Sunil as she narrated the story to him when he woke up later that afternoon.

"Don't be silly," he said. "It's only science-fiction. The writer must have had a whale of a time, letting his imagination go wild."

"Is it possible?" she repeated to Aakash in the night when she spoke to him on the telephone.

"I guess it will happen sometime in the near future, Anju," said Aakash. "There is actually already a lot of research going on in this area."

"You mean we might actually be able to freeze life, and then revive it many years later?"

"Yes," said Aakash. "It might turn out to be a way of preserving endangered species, and reviving them close to the point of extinction!"

The following Sunday Anjali sat and watched the second film. This fascinated her even more. "Boys From Brazil" was a Gregory Peck, Lawrence Olivier starrer, which had her engrossed right till the end. It was about a fanatical Nazi doctor who had survived the war and was, many years later, attempting to clone Adolf Hitler. He had managed to acquire skin and blood samples of Hitler, and was using these as DNA, so that he could recreate the Fuehrer in every respect. In fact, the crazy doctor wanted to make many such clones, so that he could turn the world into one run by Hitler clones.

Seeing her fascination, Aakash did some hunting in book shops and found a book for Anjali to read. He gave it to her when he was driving her back from the hospital in his 'Dinky'.

"I know you love to read," said Aakash as he passed her the book written by David Rorvik.

Anjali opened it and put it to her nose.

"What's that?" asked Aakash.

"Just a habit I've had from childhood," answered Anjali. "I always smell a book before I read it. In fact, I'm pretty sure I can tell you how good a book is, just by smelling it!"

"And…" prompted Aakash.

"Oh, this one's going to be great," said Anjali, catching on, at once.

David Rorvik's book: "In His Image – Towards Cloning of a Man" turned out to be so engrossing, that Anjali was riveted to it through the night. An early sleeper on normal days, she kept her bedside lamp on till 4:00 in the morning, when she finally finished the book. Even after that, although she switched off the lights, she lay on the bed in the dark, with Sunil snoring beside her, but with her mind on the extraordinary claims which Rorvik had made in the book.

At 7:00 am, she called up Aakash. "I want you to drive me to *Chikitsa* today," she said. "Can you pick me up at 9:00?"

"What's happened?" asked Aakash. "No car?"

"The car is there, Aakash. It's just that I desperately need to talk to you."

For the hour or so that it took for the drive to the hospital, Anjali spoke almost continuously, telling Aakash about the book. She was like a child who had read a fascinating story, and who wanted to share it with a friend.

"Rorvik claims this is a true story," said Anjali. "He claims that about five years before he wrote the book, a very rich businessman gave him a lot of money to find and setup a team of scientists who could create a clone of him."

"Where was this?" asked Aakash.

"He doesn't say where," answered Anjali. "He claims to have created a lab at a secret location and that the scientists after just a few years of experimentation implanted a specially prepared body-cell nucleus into the cytoplast of a human ovum. They then used this egg on a surrogate mother, who gave birth to a cloned child nine months later."

"Unbelievable," said Aakash.

"Aakash, do me a favour. Do some reading for me. I want to know more about genetics and cloning."

Aakash did just that. He spent the next few days poring over whatever journals he could lay his hand on, which carried papers on cloning.

He told her about Dolly, the sheep, who had been so much in the news a couple of years ago.

"You know, Anju, sheep have been cloned before this too. But they used to be from embryonic cells."

"And that wasn't considered all that much of a breakthrough?" asked Anjali.

"No, it wasn't," Aakash replied. "Dolly's birth in 1996 gave us the first clone created from a cell taken from an adult mammal.

He told her all about the Human Genome Project.

"The project began about nine years ago," said Aakash. "1990 to be precise."

"What do they aim to do?" asked Anjali.

"They will be aiming to understand the genetic mapping of the human species," Aakash told her. "They plan to map the nucleotides contained in a haploid reference human genome."

"I guess it will be a massive task."

"Yes," replied Aakash. "You know that the genome of every individual is unique."

"Except in the case of identical twins," added Anjali.

"And cloned organisms," continued Aakash. "So mapping the human genome will involve sequencing multiple variations of each gene."

"Where are they doing all this?"

"Oh, not in one place," said Aakash. "Although the project began at the US National Institute of Health, there are a lot of scientists working on it across the world – in Canada, New Zealand, Britain …."

"… and in India?" asked Anjali.

"None that I know of," said Aakash. "Why don't you get involved?"

"I want to, Aakash," Anjali replied. "I really want to."

The conversations she had with Aakash egged her on, and in the next few weeks, Anjali spent a lot of time at libraries and research centres in Delhi, reading up about genetics in general, and human genetics in particular.

She read about the parallel project, outside of the government, being done by Celera Corporation.

"I'm very impressed by the boss of Celera Genomics," Anjali mentioned to Aakash. "Craig Venter was actually a scientist at the National Institute of Health when the Human Genome Project started. Now he's heading Celera, and he claims that Celera Genomics will spend only 300 million dollars on the project, while the HGP budget is three billion dollars!"

"Wow, that's a tenth of the budget," exclaimed Aakash. "Are they using some other methods in the research?"

"Yes," said Anjali. "I believe they are using a riskier technique called Whole Genome Shotgun Sequencing."

"I have an idea, Anju," said Aakash. "Why don't you write to Craig Venter and suggest that you want to get involved in their project?"

"Coincidently Mr. Anand, I was thinking of exactly the same thing!"

Anjali wrote out quite a detailed letter to Celera Genomics, expressing not only her interest in being involved in the project, but also with a suggestion that she would be able to put together a team of scientists and doctors who would be very keen to contribute to the project.

She got no reply to her letter.

The twist in the tale was that just about three weeks later, Anjali received a mail from a scientist called Peter Jenkings, who was working in a laboratory in England. The innocuous looking envelope was lying on her bed when she returned from work one day. With the marking of 'Sanger Institute' on it, she looked at it curiously, wondering who it was from, and what it was about, before she picked up a paper cutter and slit open the envelope. She pulled out a long, four page, typewritten letter from it.

Peter Jenkings was a scientist working at the Sanger Institute, close to Cambridge. He introduced himself in the letter and then went on to apologise to Anjali that he had happened to chance on her letter to Celera Genomics while he was there for some discussions. From the second page onwards, Peter explained to her what the Sanger Institute was all about. Anjali read on, interested in what he was leading to.

It started as a small institute in 1992 to provide a focus for mapping, sequencing and decoding the human genome. The next year, its small group of seventeen employees moved into the location where the institute was now housed – Hinxton Hall, a 55 acre estate located about 15 kilometers south of Cambridge. In the last eight years of course, it had grown considerably and now has close to 400 employees.

Sanger Institute had been a key player in the field of genomics and lays claim to having driven many of the advances. In the recent past it had been actively involved in increasing the output of finished DNA sequences, and had become the leading contributor to the Human Genome Project.

After dwelling on the kind of research in which he himself had been involved, Peter came to the point. He was looking for clinicians to join his team, and would Anjali be willing to be part of it?

What Peter was offering her was a six month all paid training at the Sanger Institute. This would be in the form of a Career Development Fellowship. The training would be very intense and he warned her that she should be prepared for an exhausting half year, if she chose to accept. At the end of the fellowship, she would have the option of joining Sanger as a researcher, or she could be part of a small research lab which Sanger was contemplating setting up in India.

With her heart pounding, Anjali reached out for the telephone and dialed Aakash's number.

"Of course you should go," said Aakash without any hesitation at all.

Anjali, on the other hand, had all sorts of doubts running through her mind. "What about this family of mine. Do you think they would agree?"

"You'll have to cajole them, convince them, emotionally blackmail them – whatever," said Aakash, "But you have to make them agree."

"What about Yogi?"

"Is he so important? In any case, I'm pretty sure you'll be better off in another hospital."

"What about Karan? Do you think he'll manage without me?"

"He's five years old, Anju. He's started going to school. He'll miss you alright, but he'll manage. Don't worry."

"What about you," asked Anjali. "Won't you miss me?"

"Ah-ha, so now you come to the point," teased Aakash. "What you're getting at is that you won't be able to stay there without me being around!"

"Shut up, Aakash!" said Anjali.

"What you mean is that I'm so-so-important to you now," Aakash continued.

"Shut up, Aakash!"

"What you are implying is that you need me around all the time," he wouldn't give up.

"Shut up, Aakash!" said Anjali. But this time she wasn't so loud.

"So, I guess if I'm not with you to hold your hand, you won't go," said Aakash.

Anjali didn't reply. There was silence on the other side.

"Hello. Are you there?" asked Aakash.

The silence continued.

"Anju, are you crying?"

Surprisingly, Sunil had no objections at all to Anjali's plans. "Wow, England!" he said. "That should be a lot of fun. I'll also come for a few days. We can go and see the London Bridge!"

"Yes, that would be nice," said Anjali.

"What are you going for?" asked Sunil.

Anjali explained her growing fascination with human genetics and went on to tell him about Craig Venter – and how her letter had led her on to Peter Jenkings.

"Oh, you're getting into that science fiction stuff," Sunil summed it all up in a shot.

Even more surprising was the fact that Devika, too, was enthusiastic about Anjali's plans. "Don't worry at all about Karan. I'll take care of him," she volunteered.

Yogi, on the other hand, threw a fit when he heard the news. "This is not what a doctor should be doing," he fumed. "You are in a great hospital – great name, great reputation. What else could you want? You've been building up your reputation as a good doctor. At your age, that is what is most important."

"But the subject fascinates me," said Anjali.

"You'll get over it very rapidly," he theorized. "Then you will want to get back to your practice. By then you would have lost out on time, lost out on your patients, and lost out on your reputation."

Yogi had the knack of being able to convince even the most astute of disbelievers. He spoke with such conviction, that Anjali's confidence in her decision wavered. "Am I taking a wrong step?" she started thinking.

Then, as every time that she would be confused about a decision, she reached for the phone and dialed Aakash's number.

"You're nuts," said Aakash. "Why do you have to discuss this with Yogi at all? He would obviously want you to stay behind. You're his most hard working doctor, you're the best, you've got a long innings ahead, blah-blah!"

"Don't be so mean to him, Aakash."

"Anyway, I've already tied up with a travel agent," Aakash continued. "He is coming to your place this evening to collect your passport and to take your signatures on the visa application."

Anjali gasped. "Aakash, I haven't even decided as yet."

"I have," said Aakash quite firmly – sort of putting an end to the discussion.

Things moved very fast after that. It was already mid-June, and the fellowship at the Sanger Institute was to commence on the seventeenth of July. That left Anjali with barely a month to wind up all her commitments. It wasn't an easy task. She had to hand over all her patients to other doctors, and conscientious that she was, Anjali needed to spend a lot of time with each patient and then with the doctor she was handing over the case to.

Yogi was sulking. He actually stopped talking to her and had started ignoring her from the day she told him that she had decided to take up the offer. And Anjali stayed away from him, not because of his sulking, but because she was quite afraid that if he got talking, he might still convince her not to go ahead with her plan.

Anjali's tickets were booked on the British Airways flight for the fourteenth of July. That would give her a couple of days at the Sanger Institute, to settle down before the grind began.

"How will you find your way?" asked Sunil very seriously one evening. "Should I come along?"

Anjali laughed. "I'm not a kid, Sunil. Don't worry."

But a little later, she was worrying herself! She had, in the last couple of years, become so dependent on Aakash, that she would go running to him for advice and suggestions on almost everything. What would she do for these six months? And while Sunil, and even Devika and Ajay, for that matter, might actually land up in Hinxton Hall, she knew there was no way that Aakash could.

As the date of her travel drew closer, she found herself spending a lot of time with Aakash. As she had resigned from *Chikitsa*, on most days they would both find time to have lunch together, or at least meet to have coffee together. In the evenings, Anjali would pull a reluctant Sunil to go across to visit the Anands, or Aakash would coax his father to accompany him to drop in at the Sharmas' place.

"You know, Aakash," said Anjali to him one day. "You actually haven't even once said that you'll miss me."

"I can't 'miss' you, Anju," replied Aakash very seriously. "You're married, so I'll have to 'missus' you!"

"God, Aakash," groaned Anjali. "That was quite a lousy one!"

14

It wasn't planned. It wasn't planned at all. It wasn't pre-empted from either side.

It just happened.

But when it happened, they both knew that it was bound to happen.

It was a Monday, and it was the thirteenth of July – a date they would both remember forever.

By mid-July, the monsoons normally are in an advanced stage over Delhi, and the scorching heat of May and June give way to heavy rains and a very humid atmosphere. The 'well-to-do' in Delhi, move from one air-conditioned place to another, travel in their air-conditioned cars, and grumble about the terrible heat when they have to walk the hundred metres or so, from the car to their homes.

But Aakash was quite content with his 'Dinky' He hated summers – somehow the heat of Delhi was something he wasn't too comfortable with. He loved the winters, when he would be most active. Summers would drain him. So, at times, the thought of buying a new car would cross his mind, but 'Dinky' was his sweetheart, and he was very monogamous as far as cars were concerned,

Aakash was driving home that day at about 1:00 in the afternoon when his cell phone rang. When he saw that the call was from Anjali, he pulled over to the side of the road.

"Hi Anju, what's up?"

"Where are you, Aakash?" asked Anjali.

"On the Ring Road," said Aakash. "I'm headed back home."

"So early today?"

"Oh, Dad's not at home," he explained. "He's gone to Chandigarh for an exhibition. So I thought I'll make some *Aloo ka Parathas* for myself. You've met Chef Aakash, haven't you?"

"Fiction!" mocked Anjali. "A safer bet would be that I make some lunch for you and bring it across."

"You've thrown a challenge at me, Anju," Aakash retorted. "You come across, and I'll serve you the best, finger-licking *parathas* in the world!"

"Done," said Anjali. "And I've got some lovely *kulfi* from Nathu's. I'll bring that along. See you in a bit."

Anjali was in the midst of some packing. She had planned this for the day, since Sunil, Ajay and Devika were away at the shop. Karan was at a friend's place for the day. She finished putting most of the stuff into the suitcase, before she called Bahadur.

"Bahadur, I'm going to Doctor Aakash's house," she told him. "I'll be back in a couple of hours. Karan is at Puneet's place. Puneet's parents will drop him here in the evening. So, no lunch for anyone. You have yours and clean up."

When she reached Aakash's house, she found him in the kitchen, looking much like a professional chef. He was wearing a white apron and a make-shift cap which he had hurriedly made out of some corrugated white paper. One *paratha* was on the *tawa*, and he was rolling another one into shape. Of course, instead of coming out circular, as parathas are meant to be, it was turning out to be an odd shape.

Anjali burst out laughing, as she opened the freezer to put the tub of *kulfi* into.

"What are you laughing at?"

"Aakash, haven't you studied geometry at school?" asked Anjali.

Aakash stepped back to look at his handiwork on the *paratha*.

"Anjali, haven't you studied geography?" he retorted.

But the *parathas* were tasty all the same, Anjali admitted later, as they ate them along with some Punjabi mango pickle and curd.

They discussed Anjali's travel plans as they ate. They spoke for a while, but then lapsed into silence, as if both were realizing that they would not be seeing each other for some time.

"We can speak to each other on the telephone, Anju," said Aakash.

Anjali pushed back her chair and went up to him. She planted a kiss on his forehead and said, "I know, but I'll miss you terribly, Aakash."

Suddenly Aakash felt a lump in his throat. He watched quietly, as Anjali went across to the freezer and took out the kulfi. She took it to the kitchen slab and pulled out two bowls to serve it in.

Aakash's mind went back to that day in Chuchundru when they had kissed. Since then, they hadn't brought it up. They probably just felt guilty about it.

Anjali had, on one occasion, said, "Aakash, what if we were to do the ultimate-ultimate. What then?"

And he had said, "No, Anju – that would be wrong. You are married, and marriage is sacrosanct. You can't get away from it."

"But these are limits and borders which we create for ourselves."

"Yes, but marriage is a contract which you sign. You are bound by it."

"Hah," said Anjali. "Contracts also have clauses which specify exceptions. Can't falling in love be an exception, Aakash. Aren't we in love, Aakash?"

"You're nuts!" was all that Aakash had said that day.

But today, as he watched her open hair – thick, black, and shimmering in the light of the kitchen, he knew that rationality would have to wait for another day.

He knew that he wasn't being rational as he got up and went towards her. "She looks so beautiful with her hair open," was all that he was thinking.

He knew he wasn't being rational as he held her close to him and brought his lips towards hers.

The serving spoon, with which she was scooping out the *kulfi*, fell from her hand, and dropped noisily on the floor.

There was *kulfi* on the kitchen floor as they kissed.

She reached out for him and clung on tightly as they kissed hungrily.

It was very garbled when she said, "God, Aakash, I'm really going to miss you," in between the kiss. But it didn't matter. Aakash seemed to understand, anyway.

When they broke apart, Aakash cupped her face in his hands and their eyes just looked at each other in silence. As if there was no need for any words – garbled, or otherwise!

And then he held her hand; and said, "come with me, Anju."

"Where?" she asked.

"To my bedroom!"

He led the way, while she walked with wooden legs.

"I'm nervous," was all that she said.

It was an hour they would both remember – in their different ways. For her, it was all in a blur, as if she was moving in a daze through something fascinating. For him it was very vivid, as if he was in control and knew what he was doing.

It was soft and tender. He was so gentle with her, as if she was too delicate to be otherwise.

He kissed her on her ears, before he took off her earrings. He kissed her on her neck, before he took off the string of small pearls which she wore so regularly. He kissed her on her arms, as he took off the bangles which she was wearing. And then he kissed her on her finger, as he took off her wedding ring.

He unbuttoned her shirt easily. And she closed her eyes as he took it off. But then he fumbled at the clasp of her brassiere – he fumbled so long that she smiled gently. It came off finally and Anjali found herself enjoying the fascinated expression on Aakash's face and the admiration in his eyes. This time, he closed his eyes, as he buried his face in her softness. She put her arms around him as they tumbled onto the bed.

It was slow, but it was passionate. As if the world had stopped, and they had all the time in the world.

They were climbing, at moments like novices, at times as if they had all the experience in the world. And when they reached the peak, they didn't have to look down – to know that they had left the rest of the world far behind!

It was Aakash who broke the blissful silence between them as they lay on the bed.

"I have something for you," he said.

He rolled over and reached for the drawer in the bedside table.

From there he took out a small box. He opened it and pulled out a chain of gold with a pendant which was in the figure of Lord Ganesh.

"It's beautiful, Aakash," said Anjali, as he gave it to her.

"You know, there's a story behind this," Aakash started. "When my dad sold his first painting, he gave me the money, and said 'son, go buy something for the person who doesn't exist in your life right now, but who you will love the most in the world'. So I bought this, and I've kept it with me quietly all these years.

"Then put it on me, Aakash," said Anjali as she sat up. The sheet fell off, but even in her nakedness, she didn't feel self-conscious in front of him. It was as if the bond between them wasn't created just then, but had existed forever.

Aakash opened the clasp of the necklace and reached behind her neck to put it on her. As he closed the clasp, the golden figure of Ganesh settled between her breasts, as if it had found a house for itself.

Aakash looked at it fondly. It swayed gently and he felt that a ray of light had reflected off it – an omen? Or was it just a bit of his imagination?

"I'll never ever take it off, Aakash," she said. "It'll make me feel you are with me all the time!"

They dressed – and then they went to the kitchen. He exclaimed "Oh, shit ...", and started laughing. She came in, behind him, and when she saw the mess, she burst out laughing too.

There was melted *kulfi* all over the kitchen slab and the kitchen floor – one full litre of it!

15

In actuality, Anjali needn't have worried. The next six months went by in such a flurry of activities, that she had no time to miss anyone at all.

The pressure of work was so enormous that she had very little time to herself. And Anjali was so fascinated by the quiet countryside and the landscaped gardens of Hinxton, that she spent whatever free time she had, in exploring the huge campus of Sanger Institute.

The campus was still in the process of coming up. It was being built as a 'green' campus, and the laboratories and research facilities were absolutely 'state-of-the-art', capable of all the research involved, especially in the Human Genome Project.

Very often, Anjali would pack some sandwiches, take her books, and sit on the banks of the River Cam, which flows on one side of the campus. The river goes on to flow through the university city of Cambridge, just a few kilometers to the north. Sitting on the side of the river, Anjali would reminisce about sitting on her father's lap and listening to his ambition of his daughter studying either at Oxford or at Cambridge.

"I've got pretty close to that, haven't I, Papa?" she said to herself.

In the campus itself, there were numerous ponds, with lots of healthy trout in each of them.

"I'm sure Aakash would have loved fishing here,' she thought.

And then there was the Hinxton Hall, which used to be a dilapidated, three hundred year old mansion, and which was now restored and converted into a modern conference centre! But then, most of the restoration was done while retaining the original structure of the hall, so that even as a conference centre, it retained its stories of the past.

She sat over a cup of coffee, with the caretaker one day, listening to the history of the place. He told her stories of how, just before the research facilities were built, an archaeological survey had uncovered evidence of an ancient civilization there. The survey had concluded that ancestors, at least five thousand years ago had lived and worked there. Lots of evidence was found of how generations had changed, and of Anglo-Saxons coming and living there. There was lots of evidence of a thriving community living there in the past. Then, there was evidence of the settlement being abandoned about eight hundred years ago.

"Wow! All this would really have fascinated Aakash," thought Anjali.

And then she smiled, as she realized that most of her thoughts would centre around Aakash.

"I really have drifted away from Sunil," she admitted to herself.

The architects had done such a good job across the Hall, that while walking through it, Anjali always thought of it as a *jugalbandi* between an ancient British mansion and a modern cutting-edge technology research centre.

There were seventeen of them undergoing the programme at Sanger – a mix of doctors, physicists, biotechnologists and even a chemical engineer. All seventeen were into this because they had got impassioned by the subject and wanted to get into research in that area. They were of differing nationalities – Greece, Malaysia, Bangladesh, Indonesia, UK, France and India. It made such an interesting mix, that the seventeen would learn as much from the debates and discussions amongst themselves, as they did from the formal training.

Their training was very application oriented. They were more into learning techniques rather than the basic research. So, while they were being exposed to mapping, sequencing and decoding the human genome and genomes of other organisms, they were working more on the laboratory techniques of DNA sequencing and sequencing genomes.

They studied the processes followed by scientists at Sanger when they had sequenced the yeast *Saccharomyces cerevisiae* with a genome of 12 million bases, and then the first animal genome, the nematode worm with a genome of 100 million bases.

Anjali listened with rapt attention as Peter Jenkings explained to them the techniques followed when he had worked with other scientists at the Sanger Institute in completing the sequencing of the first human chromosome, Chromosome 22, in December 1999.

And now Peter continued to be involved in the Human Genome Project. Scientists at Sanger were contributing very substantially to the project, and at the end, were expected to contribute about one-third of the sequence.

"Isn't it remarkable," Peter asked the group one day, "that it was as recently as 1953, that man discovered the structure of DNA, which is really the code of instructions for all life on earth, and now, less than 50 years later, we are at the verge of sequencing the human genome !"

Anjali seemed to be in awe of Peter Jenkings almost all the time.

"I become like a small kid in front of him," she told Aakash on the telephone. "There's so much to learn from him, and he teaches in a way that learning is so much fun."

"I'm so glad you are enjoying it," said Aakash. "And I hope your enthusiasm really takes you places."

Although they had thought they would be able to chat a lot on the telephone, it didn't really work out that way. For one, it was working out very expensive. On top of this, Anjali had to call Sunil regularly too. And that call would always be endless, listening to stories about relatives or about how Bahadur was misbehaving, with Anjali not being there. Devika would also want to talk, and Anjali had little time to listen to the mundane chatter. Of course, Anjali loved those short spells with Karan – but he was always busy with his friends and the short spells with Karan always turned out to be really short!

More often than not, Aakash would call her. When he did, Anjali always had so much to talk about that she would invariably mix up everything, and have a very unsatisfied feeling at the end of the conversation.

It was early October when Anjali decided to take the test.

The kit lay in front of her, and a chill ran through her body. She did realize that although it had started becoming fairly chilly at Hinxton, the chill running through her at that moment was more out of her apprehension. For quite a few days now, Anjali knew that she needed to get the test done, but then partly because of the work pressure, and partly because of her apprehension, she kept postponing it.

She took the test – and when the result indicated positive, she just sat quietly on her bed. She was too numb to understand what it meant or how it would affect her life. Even after sitting quietly for more than an hour, she realized that she hadn't been thinking of anything at all; she had just been blank.

She then took a deep breath, pulled the telephone towards her, and dialed Aakash's number.

"Aakash, I'm pregnant ….," she said stoically.

"Wow," said Aakash. "Hey, congratulations Anju. Sunil must be thrilled."

"Aakash, this is your child !" she exclaimed.

And then there was silence on the phone for a long time – for a very, very long time. For Aakash, it took that time for the news to sink in. For Anjali, she just waited, not knowing how to react to Aakash's silence.

"You can't be serious," said Aakash finally.

Anjali told him about her symptoms and how she had sort of expected this, but had kept postponing checking it. Finally she had gone to the drug store and picked up a pregnancy test kit. It had taken just a couple of minutes to confirm her pregnancy.

"I know I can't be sure, Aakash," she said, "but my gut feeling is that this is our child."

That evening, for the first time since she had come to Sanger, Anjali didn't go to work in the laboratory. She just sat quietly in her room, letting her thoughts pendulum between elation and worry, until she drifted into sleep.

That evening for the first time in many years, Aakash cancelled his clinic. He just picked up Dinky and went on to the NH-8, driving towards Jaipur, without really knowing where he was going.

16

There are four standard nucleotide bases – adenine, thymine, guanine and cytosine. Scientists, more lovingly, call them A, T, G and C respectively. They have a sugar and phosphate base – and are capable of connecting to each other in a string-like formation, as well as pairing with other types of nucleotides, so that two strings connect parallel to each other in a double helix, somewhat like a ladder. The base pairs form the ladder's rungs and the sugar and phosphate molecules form the vertical sides of the ladder. Nucleotides are then the basic unit of DNA, or deoxyribonucleic acid, which is the hereditary material in human beings. Nearly every cell in a person's body has the same DNA. And the DNA can replicate – make copies of itself. In fact, when cells divide, each new cell has an exact copy of the DNA in the old cell.

The full DNA sequence of an organism is called a genome. The human genome contains three billion nucleotide bases, with an average gene consisting of three thousand bases. But the average is just for records – the largest known human gene is dystrophin, which has 2.4 million bases.

"When we started working on the Human Genome Project," said Peter, "we expected the total number of genes to be around a hundred and twenty thousand. But now, we estimate this figure to be just a quarter of that."

The human genome is stored on 23 chromosome pairs. There are two copies of each of the chromosomes 1 to 22 in both females and males. And then there is the 23rd chromosome, which is the sex chromosome – there are two copies of the X chromosome in females, but in males there is a single X chromosome and a Y chromosome.

"It's so ironic," thought Anjali. "In India, when a female child is born, they always say it's the mother's bad luck. But in actuality, it's the chromosomes in the father's sperm which determine the sex of the child!"

It was early December – already very cold, but in the laboratory, even at 11:30 in the night, Anjali was very warm – excited at the Dideoxy sequencing that she was doing along with Georges, the biologist from France. They were using an enzematic procedure to synthesise DNA chains of varying lengths. Slowly, very carefully, they were stopping DNA replication at one of the four bases, and then they were determining the resulting fragment lengths. Their apparatus contained four sequencing reaction tubes, one each for the A,T,G and C bases. They were using a DNA template, and Anjali had fed-in a DNA polymerase to initiate the synthesis of a new strand of DNA. She then used four deoxynucleotide triphosphates to extend the DNA strand – and then a dideoxynucleotide triphosphate to terminate the growing chain.

The fragments of varying lengths were then separated by electrophoresis.

It was six am when they finished. Anjali was tired and hungry, so she gladly said yes when Georges suggested that they drop in at the all-night cafeteria for a coffee and a donut before getting back to their rooms.

In any case, Anjali could barely catch an hour's sleep, before getting back to an important session on the anticipated benefits of genome research on forensic science.

The talk was given by a forensic expert who had strayed into the field of genetics, and got fascinated by it. He was basically giving an insight into the way in which forensic science could benefit from the ongoing genomic research. He spoke about how small bits of evidence left at the scenes of crime could be utilized to identify suspects by matching the DNA. He told them how advances in genetics were helping in identifying victims of disasters, where, in the normal course, it might be impossible to identify bodies.

The talk went on to establishing paternity and other family relationships. That was when Anjali's mind switched off from the presentation and went off to planning something else.

That afternoon she did some research of a different kind, and located an agency called Genetic Testing Laboratory in East Sussex. She spoke to them on the telephone, and she had so many questions, that it was a fairly long conversation she had with them.

"I'm so sorry, I'm carrying on with so many questions ...," she said rather hesitatingly.

"Don't worry sweetie," said the lady at the other end. "In a profession like this, there always are many things to clear up before you decide."

Then at about 7:00 in the evening, when she was sure that Aakash would be taking a break for lunch, back in Delhi, Anjali rang him up.

"Serious discussion, Aakash ....," she warned before starting.

"So, what's new, Anju?" said Aakash.

"Shut up Aakash; don't be a louse," she said. "Anyway, just be quiet, listen to what I say – and then in the end, just agree with what I want to do."

"Okay, ma'am," said Aakash obligingly.

"Aakash, I want a paternity test done," she said.

"But how? Before the baby's born?" asked a bewildered Aakash.

Anjali explained to him about the Prenatal Paternity Testing Kit from GTL, its confidentiality and how easy it would all be. One just needed to get the kit, follow a set of instructions and send the required samples back to them for the test.

"I'll have to mail you the swab to get your sample," said Anjali.

"And what if the test comes negative?" asked Aakash.

"It won't," said Anjali, relieved that at least Aakash wasn't going to object to it. "Just shut up and listen to what I'm saying."

"It'll be a sterile swab with a large Q-tip," Anjali continued. "You'll need to just swab the inside of your cheeks, and then put the swab back in a special envelope and send it back to me."

"And what'll my DNA be compared with?" asked Aakash. "...Yours? There's no way it'll match!"

"You're hardly talking like a doctor, Aakash," chided Anjali. "They would need to do an Amniocentesis procedure on me, so that they can pick up cells from the fluid in the womb."

"Why do you want to go through all this, Anju?" Aakash suddenly became serious. "What do you want to achieve? Why do you want to know?"

"I want to know, Aakash," said Anjali. "Actually, I know – but I want to be sure."

"If you know, then why don't you just leave it at that?"

"No, Aakash," said Anjali with finality. "I'm sure even you want to know. So I'm going ahead – and so are you."

"Won't it cost a bomb?" Aakash tried a different approach.

"Yes it will – but I've managed to make some contacts through one of the clinicians who's doing this programme with me. So most of it will be done at nominal cost."

"And what about the Amniocentesis?" asked Aakash.

"I've fixed that too," said Anjali. "There's a very good gynaecologist up at Cambridge, who will do the procedure for me gratis. It's quick and very safe – so you needn't worry."

"My, my – someone's become very resourceful all of a sudden!" exclaimed Aakash.

"Someone's taught me all that, hasn't he?" she retorted.

The very next day Peter Jenkings broke the news that he was resigning from Sanger Institute.

The world of genetics had started revolving around Peter, as far as Anjali was concerned – and the news of his resignation came as a special shock to her. She didn't know why he was resigning, and this added to her confusion. She spoke to others in the group with her, but they too, had no clue about the reasons.

Peter himself remained so busy over the next few days, that Anjali and the rest didn't have an opportunity to discuss the resignation with him.

It was only about a week later, while they were working in the lab at around 10:00 in the night, that he called eight of them into his cabin.

"I have something very important to put forth to you," he began.

The hush in the room was almost palpable.

"You must be wondering why I've called just the eight of you," Peter continued.

Anjali glanced at Haseena, the physicist from Bangladesh and at Zainal from Malaysia, but they looked as blank as she was.

"I've been at Sanger for more than five years now," said Peter. "I've been deeply involved in some of the projects going on here. And so it's with quite a heavy heart that I'm saying goodbye."

Peter paused, as if to gauge the reactions of those in front of him.

"I'm not leaving because I wish to get into some other world," he continued. "Actually I'm going to be moving in the same direction, but in a slightly different path – a path which I personally feel will be shorter and quicker to the goals which I wish to achieve."

No one still asked any questions.

"The best part is that I'm getting a lot of support in what I'm getting into. There's a foundation which is providing half the funding, and the other half comes from a very rich Briton of Indian origin – Lord Krish Mehra, who came and settled here in the 1960s."

Anjali listened on with keen interest.

"And so I'm setting up – in fact, have already set up, another genomic research institute. It's called the JGI – the Jenkings Genomics Institute. Lord Mehra had gifted us some land for this about a year back – just west of Manchester – at a place called Hale Barns. The institute is up and running already, although it's been under wraps till now. Officially it gets inaugurated next Monday."

Anjali's fascination for the man quadrupled in those few minutes. "I always knew he was highly respected for his work," thought Anjali. "But now I know he's got so much drive in him, that I wouldn't be surprised to see him getting a Nobel Prize a few years down the line!"

Peter went on to tell them about the research equipment already installed at the JGI and the work which had commenced. Anjali could make out that while their general research seemed to be in the same direction as Sanger's, JGI's research appeared to focus more on the practical uses of the research findings in the field of genetics so far.

"Actually," thought Anjali, "I'd love to work there!"

The coffee machine in the corner of Peter's cabin was now making gurgling noises, indicating that it was ready for some action too. All nine of them in the room obliged it as they trooped up and filled up their mugs. Then they settled down once again on the sofas, pretty much ready for the long night ahead, which they had already sensed.

"JGI is going to focus its research on Embryonic Stem Cells," Peter announced. "As you all know, Adult Stem Cells can only differentiate into different cell types of their tissues of origin. The big advantage of Embryonic Stem Cells is that they are pluripotent, which means that they can differentiate into any of the three germ layers – endoderm, mesoderm, or ectoderm. In other words, they can develop into each of the more than two hundred cell types of the adult body when they are stimulated for a specific cell type."

Anjali's mind went back to what she had learnt about Embryonic Stem Cell lines – cultures of cells derived from the ebiplast tissue of a blastoplast, which is an early stage embryo, about 4-5 days old in humans, and which consists of around a hundred cells.

Peter continued. "And we're going to do a lot of work on therapeutic cloning – creating genetically identical cells for tissues and organs for transplantation, so that there would be little or no immune response. Both of you doctors here, Anjali and Derrik, would tell us that this would be of such great help in transplant surgery, where there is a need for large amounts of immune-suppressive drugs, which then cause a lot of unwanted side-effects and risks. They also interact with other medicines and affect their metabolism."

It was well past midnight when Peter Jenkings came to the point.

"What I'm offering the eight of you, is that you move along with me to the JGI," said Peter. "You all get over with your fellowships at Sanger at the end of this month. I am suggesting, firstly, that we extend your stay in England by another month, which you spend at JGI."

All eight of them now looked at each other – confused, but excited at the same time – very, very excited.

Peter didn't wait for their excitement to abate.

"Beyond that, at JGI we want to set up small research centres in various countries. If any, or all of you, feel up to it, we would welcome an association. For example, Lord Mehra has already indicated that he would be very keen to additionally fund a research centre in India – so Anjali, you could take a call on that."

Very obviously, none of the eight slept at all that night, even after getting back to their rooms.

Anjali of course, called Aakash as soon as she got back, and discussed the offer with him.

"You must go ahead, Anju," said Aakash. "But first, have a chat with the gynae friend of yours, and make sure that it'll be okay for you to continue. Then you must probe a little more to check on the 'how's' and the 'why's' of the centre being planned in India."

Then she had a chat with Sunil. Anjali was quite relieved when he too agreed that she should go ahead with the additional one month at Manchester.

The very day after they completed their fellowship at the Sanger Institute, all eight of them were on a mini-coach heading from Cambridge to Manchester.

Anjali thought she would relax during the drive, and probably catch up with some sleep. But she was wrong. The beautiful countryside, covered in a lot of places with freshly fallen snow, only added to the excitement of the thought of being back at work with Peter Jenkings.

When they reached, they went straight to the laboratories. Peter looked as excited as they were, as he took them to show them the facilities. And all of them were quite surprised. They had expected to see equipment still in packed condition – and the labs still being set-up. What they actually saw, was a scaled down version of the labs in which they had been working at Sanger. Obviously the labs had been in the making for a while – and some of the staff working there were into similar research as what was going on at the Sanger Institute.

"So, is JGI also going to contribute to the Human Genome Project?" asked Zainal.

"Not really," said Peter. "Not in the genetic mapping, anyway. We've moved a bit ahead."

Where they were staying, wasn't anywhere as comfortable as the rooms they had at Sanger. Actually, they were put up in houses which had been converted into guest rooms. And they were doubled up in the rooms – Anjali was with Haseena. But none of them even gave it a thought. They knew they had just a month more to extract knowledge from that huge bank which they called Peter Jenkings.

They had had many discussions in the last five months, but somehow, the issue of ethics in genetic research never came up. For Anjali, it came up two weeks later, when Peter was guiding her in some laboratory work on Telomeres.

Telomeres are pieces of DNA that protect the ends of chromosomes. They shorten as cells divide, and are therefore considered a measure of ageing in cells.

The experiment they were doing was a part of a series which was leading them to find conditions in which Telomeres don't shorten as cells divide.

"So we might end up controlling ageing in humans?" asked Anjali incredulously.

"That's right," said Peter.

Peter asked Anjali to do her own research into Telomeres. As she carried on with the experiments, she did a lot of reading – and pored over a few published journal papers in that area.

"Peter, I know the lab is close to a breakthrough in this," said Anjali a couple of days later. "But doesn't the steady shortening of Telomeres with each replication in body cells have a role in the prevention of cancer?"

"Possibly," was Peter's cryptic answer.

"Then wouldn't it be ethically wrong to continue experimenting on shortening of Telomeres?"

"Ethics, Anjali?" asked Peter. "We're into science. Let's just work on that – and leave ethics and ethical questions to philosophers."

"But this is a natural process, Peter," argued Anjali. "Would it be right to interfere with natural ageing?"

They discussed for a while, but then Anjali got the feeling that Peter was getting irritated, and so she kept quiet, even though she was a bit disturbed.

"Maybe I'm wrong," she thought later. "I guess the role of science is to discover. How it's used is a different aspect."

But while she wasn't too convinced herself, she decided to leave it at that.

They were all called for the New Year eve party at Lord Mehra's house – an inspiring, palatial house, with a huge lawn. There weren't too many people invited – just the eight of them, and some of the 'who's-who' of Manchester. There were a couple of barbeques set-up on the lawn – and drinks were flowing freely.

Anjali picked up a glass of Baccardi, but before she took a sip, she changed her mind and put it back. She picked up a glass of wine instead, and smiled to herself as she remembered the couple of times on which she had argued with Aakash over her love for an occasional drink.

"I don't like women drinking," he had said.

"But why?" Anjali had argued. "If you don't mind men drinking, then why should you mind women doing the same?"

"I don't know." Aakash had taken the glass of whiskey away from her and replaced it with a Coke. "No logical reason, but to me, it's not feminine."

"What nonsense," said Anjali. "That's just male chauvinism!"

But she had continued with the Coke, all the same.

Peter came towards her.

"Oh, there you are," he said. "I've been looking for you. Let's go across and meet Krish."

There was still an hour to go before midnight. Lord Mehra was sitting along with three other scientists when Peter led Anjali up to him. Somehow, she had expected him to be a haughty type of person, and so she was pleasantly surprised when he spoke to her in Hindi. She immediately felt relaxed.

They quickly got down to business. Susan Hutton, one of the scientists in the group, who Anjali later learnt was a colleague of Peter's at JGI, was the one who led the discussion.

She told them about how the British government was being very restrictive in permitting research on therapeutic cloning.

"But why?" asked Anjali. "It'll be so beneficial if we are able to make breakthroughs in so many areas which are still 'gray' areas to us."

"Exactly," agreed John, the other geneticist in the group. "The restrictions are based on ethical reasons – how can man play God, and such like."

"But ultimately, if we can help people, then why not?" said Peter.

"Yes," said Susan. "To those who argue against interfering with nature, I say – then why did we allow scientific development of drugs? Isn't that interference with nature, too?"

"And so," said Peter, "we've decided to set-up small laboratories in different locations across the world, where we can do some research which might not be permitted here."

"It would also bring in some diversity into our experiments," added John.

Lord Mehra now turned to Anjali. "Which is why, Dr. Sharma, I've suggested that we set up a lab in India. And Peter has indicated - in fact insisted - that we ask you to lead the laboratory in India."

Anjali glanced gratefully at Peter, but waited for them to continue. Lord Mehra did.

"I know for certain that Indian laws on genetic research are not so restrictive – not as yet, anyway. So let's take this as an opportunity to move ahead."

They discussed the possible size of the lab, and some broad areas in which research could be focused on, in the India lab of JGI. The lab was being planned with a strength of five researchers, including Anjali, and about ten support staff. And Anjali was delighted when she learnt about the equipment which they were planning for the lab. Obviously, Lord Mehra was being more than generous with his money, for the project.

"We would focus on certain aspects of therapeutic cloning," said Peter. "And then we could delve in other areas as we move along."

"I'm excited," said Anjali.

Peter continued. "Susan and I would hand-hold for the first few years, and we'll help in locating the right staff."

Lord Mehra looked towards Anjali. "The location is going to be important. We definitely don't want to look at a big city like Delhi. We'd rather look for a quiet place, and where the weather is moderate – somewhere in north-east India, for example?"

"Whoops !" thought Anjali. "This is going to be tough. Sunil will never let me stay alone. And with the baby…?"

The sudden bursting of balloons and the cheering and toasting brought her mind back to the party – and to the realization that 2001 had been ushered in.

Anjali overslept the next day. From the party, Haseena went off to a relative's place in downtown Manchester. Anjali had got to bed well past 2:00 am, and with her mind in a muddle, she had slept rather fitfully. She had set the alarm for 8:00 am – but had slept through the twenty seconds of a persistent attempt by the alarm clock to ring her out of her sleep.

It was around 11:00 am, as the courier boy rang the bell for the third time, when she tumbled out of the bed.

Groggily, Anjali signed the receipt, put on the kettle for a cup of tea, and then went to wash her face. It was only when she had made the tea, and settled down in the armchair to sip it, did she pick up the envelope from the table.

The tea almost spilled as Anjali realized that it was the Paternity Test report from the Genetic Testing Laboratory. With shaking hands, she tore open the envelope.

Anjali looked at the clock and did a quick calculation. It would be around 4:30 am in India. Her hesitation lasted just a couple of seconds, and then she pulled the telephone towards her. She dialed Aakash's number and woke him up.

She just had to share the news with him!

17

No one really knew how the fire started.

It was a typical January night in Delhi. The temperature must have been around five degrees Celsius. But in that street in Kashmere Gate, with a dozen or so *chowkidars* lighting up small bonfires to keep themselves warm, it was very easy for the fire to have gone unnoticed for quite a while. Very often, the *chowkidars* would use old tyres and waste rubber material from the spare parts' shops as material to burn. They didn't mind the smoke because they felt that in the winters, the smoke stays low, and acts like a blanket, insulating them from the cold, and from the dew which collects on everything early in the morning. With all the smoke and the smell from the plastic, wood and rubber being burnt on the street, the fire in the Sharma Motor Parts shop was not noticed until it was too late anyway.

It probably started as a short circuit within the shop itself.

Sharma Motor Parts was an imposing shop in Kashmere Gate, spread over three floors. After the renovations which Sunil had personally supervised, the shop was very swanky, especially when compared to the other shops in the area. Sunil had got the entire inventory computerized and it was one of the few shops where it took just a few moments to get the stock position of a spare part, its location and its cost. The result was a better stock position, and a very large inventory, which naturally then, drew a larger horde of customers to them, than to the neighbouring shops.

For the flames, however, all this was irrelevant. They grew every second, devouring everything that came their way. Everything non-metallic was burnt to cinders. Even metallic stuff in the shop couldn't stand the scorching heat as the fire became an inferno, and melted into unrecogniseable lumps of waste.

It would have been around 2:00 am when one of the *chowkidars* finally noticed thick smoke billowing out of the building. He ran to the next lane to alert the *chowkidar* there. They spent a bit of time confused, not really knowing what to do, realizing at once that the fire was well beyond the 'buckets of water' stage. Finally they called up the fire station.

By the time the fire tenders arrived, the fire had been raging for almost two hours. The intensity of the fire was so obvious that the firemen immediately decided to focus on preventing the fire from spreading to adjoining buildings, rather than on trying to save Sharma Motor Parts.

When the *chowkidar* located Ajay's cell phone number and rang him up, it was around 4:30 am.

"Who is it, Ajay?" asked Devika, rather irritated at being disturbed at that unearthly hour.

"Rajesh, the street *chowkidar* at the shop," Ajay replied. "He was rather incoherent, but I gather there's a fire in our shop. He wants me to come there."

"Now?" asked Devika.

"Yes. Coming?"

"No. I'm sleepy – you take Sunil and go.

The gravity of the situation hit them only when they reached Kashmere Gate. It was still dark, but they could see the columns of smoke from a few kilometers away."

"Oh my God!" exclaimed Ajay, as they reached the lane, which had now been cordoned off by the police.

For a long time the two brothers watched helplessly as they realized that even after the fire was doused, there would hardly be anything left of the shop. They moved as close to the shop as the policemen would allow them to, and then they sat, defeated, on the pavement of the street just watching the firemen fighting the fire.

The sun came up slowly, lighting up the whole place and making the devastation in the street more and more clear, just as if to leave no doubt at all in Ajay and Sunil's minds. Slowly the crowds started gathering. The number of curious onlookers swelled, and the police had a job at hand.

At about 7:30 am the owner of one of the shops in the adjacent street – an elderly Sardarji called Mr. Harbans Singh, came up to them with two cups of tea. He sat silently next to them, as if offering sympathy, which didn't really need any words.

"I hope the insurance company settles the claims quickly," he said finally.

The cup of tea fell from Ajay's hand. He suddenly remembered that their insurance policy had lapsed three days ago, and that Devika was planning to shift their policy to another company since their premium was turning out to be much lower.

Ajay was shivering when he pulled out his cell phone and called up Devika.

"Have you paid the premium for the shop's insurance?" he asked her.

"No, the agent was busy the whole of last week," said Devika. "But he's coming in at 11:00 this morning."

"You can tell him to forget about it," Ajay almost yelled as he disconnected the phone.

And then he cried. He pulled out his handkerchief and sobbed into it. Sunil looked on stoically for a while. But then he too, couldn't control himself as he clung on to his brother for support. The elderly Sardar Harbans Singh held both their hands and consoled them.

"Have faith my sons," he said in Punjabi. "Have faith in the one above – for only He knows what's best."

The devastated family sat in the living room of their house that evening. None of the three – Ajay, Devika and Sunil – knew what lay ahead for them. Karan was too young to really comprehend what had happened. All he knew was that something very serious was amiss, and he longed for his mother to be there.

"She would have known how to sort things out," he thought to himself.

Devika had suddenly become a very subdued person. She realized the big mistake she had made, in trying to save a couple of thousand Rupees through the promise of lower premiums. For a change, she sat quietly. And for a change, the decibel levels in the Sharma household were very low – in fact they were close to zero!

For the first time in the last five and a half months that Anjali had been away, Sunil was missing her. He was missing her terribly.

"She knows how to act in situations like this," he said to Aakash, when he and his father came to visit them the next day.

Aakash agreed. "Don't worry," he said. "She'll be back in a week's time."

Sunil had spoken to Anjali on the telephone at least five times since the fire. But she was not in the picture of the whole situation, and couldn't really offer any advice. To add to it, the shock of the lapse in the insurance was overbearing.

"I don't believe this, Sunil," she said. "How could all three of you slip up on a simple thing like insurance?"

"*Bhabi* used to handle all that, Anjali," said Sunil. "I guess Ajay and I somehow took it for granted that it must have been done."

As if to add fuel to the fire, just three days after the actual fire, the owner of the shop, from whom the Sharmas had taken it on rent, demanded compensation from them.

"But it not our fault," argued Ajay. "Besides, we've lost everything in the fire!"

"That doesn't concern me," said the owner. "You should have built in safety devices and a fire warning system in the shop. I'm going to file a legal case against you."

That was when Aakash's father, who along with Aakash, was sitting at the Sharmas' residence when the call came, advised them to move away from Delhi as soon as they could.

"But how can we?" asked Ajay. "We have nothing with us now. All our money was invested in the business. Our bank balance may last us for six months – a year at most. What then? And where do we go? All we now own is this house!"

When they went back home, Aakash's father discussed what came to his mind with Aakash. They owned two big houses and a school, all in Shillong – all of which were actually owned by Aakash's step-mother – his father's second wife – and which were transferred to his father after they had got married.

When she had passed away, Aakash and his father had both decided that they didn't want to live there and had moved to Delhi. The school was shut down and all three properties were locked up. Neither of them had even seen the properties in the last nine years, except on one visit which Mr. Anand had made to check on their status and to hire new caretakers.

18

Aakash had always been in love with Shillong. In the two years that he had spent there, the city had grown on him. He would, in fact, have loved to have continued staying in Shillong.

It all started when Aakash was turning thirty. After about six years of running a private practice, he had decided to do his MD, and had taken up paediatrics as a specialization. It was in the fifteen day break which he had in between the two years of the MD programme, that his father took him for a well deserved holiday to Shillong.

A good friend of Mr. Anand, who was then the Commanding Officer of the Air Force Station at Laitkor peak, had invited them as his personal guests. They had a beautifully set-up guest suite in the officers' mess all to themselves, and Aakash and his father decided that they must go all-out to enjoy themselves.

Group Captain Kamal Kant Dwivedi, the Commanding Officer, was a tall, well-built man with an impressive personality. Together, he and Mr. Anand made a beautiful pair of friends. Although they were meeting after a gap of almost five years, to others it appeared as if they had spent all their time together.

"We guys here work hard in the day," said Dwivedi. "And then we party even harder in the evenings."

So Aakash and his father would spend the days exploring the city and the evenings with the officers of the Air Force Station, drinking and dancing till late in the night.

One evening, Gp. Capt. Dwivedi and his wife, Ranjana, took them along to a party at the house of a local minister. Mr. Richmond Blah was an old hand at politics in the state of Meghalaya and was, in some circles, considered to be as influential as the Chief Minister himself.

That was when they met Richmond Blah's sister, Jennah.

And that's when Aakash's father and Jennah fell in love with each other at first sight.

"It was all so copy book style," Aakash would tell his father later. "So much like a scene from a Mills & Boon novel!"

"At my age, son, it's either that, or not at all," his father had replied.

Aakash wondered how many men would ever have had the chance to say, "look, my dad's falling in love!" He bent over and whispered just that into Ranjana's ear. She took it on from there, got someone to put on Frank Sinatra's 'Strangers in the Night...' on the music system, and ignited the evening.

Jennah and Mr. Anand discovered that they were both painters, that they both enjoyed cooking, and that they both could actually fall in love at first sight.

What followed then, was a whirlwind romance. In the next six months Mr. Anand found that he had enough work in Shillong to warrant three or four trips there, and Jennah found that Delhi was just the place for her painting exhibitions.

A year later, they were married – Mr. Anand was fifty three and Jennah was thirty five, but so what!

Aakash got a big kick out of distributing the wedding cards.

"Please do come for the wedding reception," he would innocently tell his friends, as he gave the cards.

"Congrats Aakash – you're getting married!"

"Oh no, not me," Aakash would say with a serious face – and would enjoy watching jaws drop as he would add, "my dad is!"

The Anands were fairly rich. But the Blahs were richer many times over. The Khasis of Meghalaya live in a matriarchal society, so very large chunks of property had been passed down from Jennah's mother to her when she had died, as Jennah was her only daughter. This included a primary school which Jennah was running and two huge bungalows – one close to the school, and another about twenty minutes drive away.

By the time his father and Jennah got married, Aakash had finished his MD in paediatrics. Father and son then moved up to Shillong – and it was a lovely happy family. They lived in the bungalow close to the school, and Aakash set up a clinic and a mini hospital for children in the other bungalow. Jennah would spend the day at the school, Aakash would spend the day at the clinic and his father became Man-Friday, shuttling between the requirements of the school and the clinic. Then in the evenings, Jennah and Mr. Anand would paint. They had set up a sort of studio in one of the rooms and they enjoyed giving ideas to each other. Aakash would sit with a book in another room, content to see them both so happy, especially after the fiasco of his father's first marriage and his unhappy memories of his parents perpetually fighting during his childhood.

In the Khasi matrilineal society, property is passed on from mother to the youngest daughter, or *khaduh*. But Jennah was so much in love with Mr. Anand, that she insisted on moving away from traditions and making sure that all her property was transferred in her husband's name. The Blahs were not too traditional, and all it took was agreements from her maternal uncles to do that. Somehow, it gave her a bit of happiness that she wasn't pulling Mr. Anand into all her traditions.

The happiness lasted just over two years. Until that morning in school, when Jennah collapsed. They rushed her to the hospital, but even before they could diagnose that she had a tumor in the brain, she died.

It all finished as suddenly as it started.

"If the Sharmas take up our offer, why don't we, too, move to Shillong," suggested Aakash to his father.

"I'm not too sure," Mr. Anand hesitated.

Since the properties were lying unused for so long anyway, they had both decided to offer one of the bungalows to the Sharmas. Mr. Anand was of the opinion that they should move out of Delhi and start life afresh.

"But why Shillong?" asked Ajay.

"As good as any other place," said Mr. Anand in a matter-of-fact way. "But seriously, it's a beautiful place, life is laid-back. There's very little stress in everyday life, and you'll probably add ten years to your life."

"All we know in life is the business we were into," said Ajay.

"So continue that," Mr. Anand advised. "Put this house on rent, and with that money, you'll probably get a pretty big shop in Shillong on rent. Then take a bank loan for the new business and start afresh in a new place. Believe you me, you won't regret it."

Aakash spoke to Anjali when she got back to her room that night.

"Just two days left, Aakash," she said excitedly. "Then I'll be back."

They had been talking very frequently since the day of the fire.

"I'm worried for all of them," Anjali had said.

"Don't worry, I've been with them as much as I can."

"I'm sure you have," said Anjali. "And I've been telling Sunil not to worry so much. I've got a job; JGI is paying well, and I'm sure it'll be enough for the family."

Aakash told her about his father's idea and the discussion they had had with Ajay, Devika and Sunil.

"Yes, Sunil spoke to me about it," said Anjali. "I thought it might be a good idea. But what about you and Uncle? I'm not going all the way to Shillong, with you in Delhi."

Aakash didn't tell her that he had already thrown the idea to his father. They spoke for a while, and then Aakash had to hang up since it was time to attend to his clinic.

He was still with his first patient when Anjali called him back again. "I need to talk to you urgently, Aakash," she said.

"Okay, give me about ten minutes," said Aakash. "I'll call you back when I'm through with this patient."

When he did, he found Anjali very excited.

"I have an idea," she started. "If this works, it might be just the thing I'm looking for."

"And what, may I ask, is that?" Aakash asked patiently.

"You have a school in Shillong, don't you?"

"It's just a building now," Aakash replied. "It used to be a school ten years ago!"

"Well, would you want to rent out that building to me?"

"You mean you now want to switch from genetics to running a

school?" asked Aakash incredulously.

"Shut up, Aakash," said Anjali. "Just keep quiet and listen – and then go and discuss it with Uncle."

Anjali continued. "You remember I told you about my meeting with Lord Mehra on new year's eve? And about his and Peter's plan to set up a lab of JGI here in India? Wouldn't Shillong be the ideal place?"

"You mean the school ..." said Aakash.

"Exactly," answered Anjali. "It would be just the right building. We could very easily set it up as a laboratory. It might ultimately grow to be bigger than their Manchester lab!"

"Well, said Aakash, "I suppose I could have a chat about it with Dad and ..."

"That's settled then," said Anjali, as if leaving no room for discussion. "Let me go and propose this to Peter."

"Hey, hold it," said Aakash, astounded at the pace of Anjali's thoughts. "Even your folks haven't taken any decision as yet!"

"Don't worry," said Anjali. "I'll convince them as soon as I am there."

And with that, she rushed off to locate Peter Jenkings.

19

Anjali was in the seventh month of her pregnancy when she landed back in Delhi. And it was showing very evidently now.

By the time she emerged from immigration, it was past 1:00 in the night. But they were all there this time – Sunil, Karan, Ajay and Devika. With their shop and their business in ashes, suddenly Anjali had become an important element in their lives. And then Aakash had added a new dimension into the turmoil in their lives by bringing in the proposal of a move to a new city. None of them were sure that Anjali would be ready for a move out of Delhi; they still thought of her as a traditional doctor – and somehow, they were convinced that *Chikitsa* and Yogi were best for her.

Devika had withdrawn into a shell since the fire, and was entirely leaving the decision of whether they should move or not, to Ajay. So now their decision was hinging on what Anjali might want to do.

And of course, Aakash was there with them at the airport to receive Anjali – a single red rose, with a small light blue tag saying

'Welcome Back', stowed away in the bag which he was carrying. He wasn't sure at all that he would get an opportunity to give the rose to Anjali.

She was amongst the first few to emerge from the passenger area of the airport. Even before Karan yelled, "Mamma…" and tugged at Sunil's shirt-sleeve to pull him forward, Aakash had already sighted her. He felt his heart miss a beat as he saw her, and then another as his eyes moved down to the bump on her.

"Whoa, boy!" he said to himself. "Missing too many beats is not good for the heart!"

Karan hugged Anjali, and then Sunil gave her a hug. Aakash saw her eyes looking at him as she hugged him back. When Devika and Ajay finished with their hugs, Aakash held out his hand.

"Welcome back, Anjali," he said.

"Oh, thank you …" she said, with a naughty little smile on her face.

To date, Anjali insists that she doesn't tell lies. But then, she also says that there is nothing wrong with half truths – those aren't lies.

So when she said, the next morning that she was going to *Chikitsa*, it wasn't a lie at all. But the whole truth was that she was looking for an opportunity to be with Aakash.

"Have you thought of a name for him?" she asked, as they drove to *Chikitsa* in her car. She had picked him up on the way, insisting that he couldn't have anything better to do in the morning, anyway.

"It's going to be a girl, Anju," replied Aakash.

"Thus spake the astrologer Aakash Anand … !" Anjali teased.

"No, seriously. Many years back, some friends and I had gone to Hoshiarpur in Punjab. There we went to an Aashram of Bhrigu Rishi. One of the astrologers there claimed to have leaves on which parts of the *Bhrigu Samhita* is written. From this, he had predicted that I would have a daughter, who would love me a lot."

"Wow," said Anjali. "You must take me there sometime."

"At that time, I had laughed," Aakash continued. "Mom and Dad's fights were fresh in my mind, and I was so sure that I would never get married."

"Okay, assuming that the astrologer's right, think of a name for her."

"I've already thought of one – Rukmani Kunjamma Devi. How's that?" said Aakash.

Anjali landed a punch on his stomach.

"Second choice?" she asked.

"Tanvi," he said.

"Tanvi – sounds nice," Anjali replied. "What does it mean?"

"Very straight and simple, it means 'delicate girl'," said Aakash.

At her place, Anjali was enjoying the new-found attention that she was getting. She wasn't sure whether it was because she had been away for so long, or because she was bearing another *chirag* of the family. Or was it because of the fire? It could also have been because of Devika's subdued attitude after her lapse in insuring the shop.

For a change, she had the attention of Devika and Ajay as she told them details about the plans of setting up the labs in the school in Shillong.

"Give it just ten years, and I'm sure it'll be acknowledged as one of the leading genetic labs in the world!" said Anjali.

"But what about the three of us?" asked Sunil. "We've been so used to a large-scale business. Will we be able to adjust to Shillong?"

"Shillong is growing very rapidly, Sunil," Anjali pointed out. "The number of cars and other vehicles has grown tremendously in the last few years. So there is bound to be a huge demand for motor spares."

"I guess we do see your point," said Ajay. "Even Aakash has been convincing us about this."

"Added to it, look at your comparative advantage," said Anjali. "You know the Delhi market so well, that setting up a business there, and then quickly taking a lead in a small-town market will be very easy for you all."

"The pace of life will be so different," moaned Sunil.

"Yes, but relax," said Anjali. "Take it easy for a change."

The discussions at the Anand household of two, were more straightforward. In their hearts, both father and son knew that they would love to go back to Shillong. If there was any hesitation, it was only in Mr. Anand's mind – an apprehension that living there again would bring back memories of those two lovely years.

"It'll hurt," he said.

"But think of it this way, Dad – Jennah would have wanted us to move back there," said Aakash. "I'll run the clinic for children once again, and you'll set up your studio again!"

"Without her…?"

"Of course you will, Dad," said Aakash encouragingly. "Haven't you got back to painting in Delhi? And Shillong is so inspirational for artists!"

"And the school…?"

"It'll be put to good use," said Aakash. "Jennah would have loved to see scientific research going on there."

20

The move to Shillong was as enjoyable as it was smooth and uneventful.

Aakash, Sunil and Ajay had made a recce trip first and during that trip itself, had located a shop in Mawlanghat in Bara Bazar, which was up for lease. They liked it so much that they paid an advance for it without even consulting Devika and Anjali.

Anjali was now in her eighth month, so she went through a round of consultations with a gynaecologist at the Safdarjung Hospital before going ahead with the journey. In fact, she had even already made contact with Dr Meena Saikia who was the head of the Gynaecology department at the Nazareth Hospital in Shillong.

They moved as one big family. The household stuff was packed in both houses in two days and then loaded on trucks. For a change, 'Dinky' was being taken for a ride. She was loaded onto another truck along with the other cars belonging to the Sharmas, and sent off, with Aakash crossing his fingers that she reaches Shillong safely.

Then they all boarded a flight to Guwahati and from there, got into two cabs for the drive to Shillong. It wasn't too long a drive – the 95 kilometers took a little over two and a half hours, and except for a stop at Nongpoh for a cup of tea, they continued straight to Shillong. But the scenic beauty made the ride so exhilarating, that by the time they reached the hotel where they had booked themselves for the first two nights, none of them had any regrets in their mind about having chosen Shillong as a place to settle down in.

They had timed themselves so that their household goods had already reached Shillong before they did. Richmond Blah made sure that they got all the help they needed, and by the end of the third day, both bungalows had already started looking like replicas of their two houses in Greater Kailash.

Anjali was not allowed out of the hotel, in spite of all her protests. She was let out only when the bungalows were all set.

The shop, on the other hand, took much longer to set up.

Both Ajay and Sunil were agreed that they would open the shop only after it was well stocked. And they went about it in a very organized way.

Aakash, through Mr. Blah, got them introduced to officials in the Road Transport Authority. With them, the two brothers did some research on the kinds of vehicles which were plying not only in and around Shillong, but also in the entire state of Meghalaya. They did a quick analysis of the expectations of growth in each of the vehicle segments, and then took decisions on the stock positions that they would want to hold in the shop.

A week later, both of them went to Delhi to place large orders for their shop. They had also done some analysis of how frequently the supplies would need to be replenished, but had agreed that they would keep these a bit flexible just in case they had gone wrong with their assessments of the uptake of spares in the market, given that there were already quite a few motor spare parts dealers in the Shillong markets.

Sharma Motor Parts opened in its new avatar a month later.

In that one month. Ajay and Sunil spent a great deal of time in Delhi tying up the supplies. During this period, Aakash would escort Anjali for her check-ups at the Nazareth Hospital.

"Aren't you going to show me a bit of Shillong at least?" asked Anjali, when they were returning from one of the visits to the hospital.

"Another few days, Anju," said Aakash. "And then there'll be lots to show you."

"No, but any one place today," insisted Anjali.

So Aakash took her to the Butterfly Museum at Riatsamthiah. He thought they would spend a half hour or so there, but they ended up spending close to two hours.

"What an exhilarating place," Anjali said excitedly. "I've played with butterflies when I was a kid, but I'm enjoying it so much even now."

She had her hand outstretched, and a multicoloured butterfly was trying to balance itself on the tip of her forefinger. Anjali held her breath, so as not to scare it away.

"Breathe, Anju," said Aakash. "These guys are bold and adventurous!"

"Shh … keep quiet, Aakash," Anjali replied, keeping absolutely still. "Let me enjoy myself."

A couple more – one large and one small – landed on her large belly and made Anjali even more stiff, as she looked down.

"Wow, that's so fascinating!" she murmured.

Aakash was laughing now, enjoying himself just watching Anjali being so thrilled at the sight of such a variety of butterflies.

"Just go away, Aakash," said Anjali. "You're spoiling my fun!"

Anjali held his hand as they walked around the museum, understanding the life cycles and the habitats of butterflies.

"How come butterflies have so many different designs on them?" asked Anjali.

"See those three guys in uniforms there?" asked Aakash. "They are the official museum designers. They catch the butterflies, paint designs on them, and then let them out."

He yelped as he got a kick on his shins for his efforts at an explanation.

Dr Meena Saikia wasn't yet on duty when Anjali was wheeled into the labour room at 6:00 in the morning. But it didn't matter; the pains were still continuing when she came in a couple of hours later.

At around 11:30, Dr Meena noticed signs of foetal distress and decided not to take a chance. She opted for delivery by caesarian section, and Anjali was moved to the operation theatre.

It was exactly 12:34 by the clock in the OT when the baby was born.

21

By the time she was three years old, it was obvious that Tanvi was going to grow up to be a very charming young lady.

After the tantrums of Karan as a child, the Sharma household was going through the experience of a delicate little girl growing in their midst. She was so soft-spoken, that they all wondered how! But even at three, Tanvi had a will of her own. She wouldn't be bullied into anything she wouldn't want to, and while the methods were different, she got her way as much as Karan did – probably even more.

She grew up amongst two adoring parents, an adoring brother, and an adoring *Tau* and *Tai* – Ajay and Devika. But still, her favourite was Aakash Uncle. She could be doing anything at all, she would just leave it all and go running to him whenever he would drop into their house.

"Aakash Uncle!" she would yell welcomingly. "Come, play with me."

And Aakash would become a little child, playing hide-and-seek with her, carrying her on his shoulders when he would take her out and making her sit on his lap as he took her for rides in 'Dinky'. Tanvi loved that the most.

"You may not realize it," said Anjali one day, "but I think she can easily claim part ownership of 'Dinky' now."

It was probably true. Tanvi would hold on to the steering wheel as Aakash would drive, imagining that she was driving. She would lean on the horn when anyone came in front, and she would move her hand down to the gear lever whenever Aakash did.

"All she needs now is a license," said Aakash.

On Tanvi's birthday, Aakash told Anjali that he wanted to take them both to Shillong Peak.

"Although an Air Force Station is located there, inside that is a sanctum, where obeisance is paid to *U Shulong*," Aakash told her.

For the first time, Aakash noticed a hesitation in her.

"You take Tanvi and go, Aakash," she said. "My folks won't like it if I go to a temple with you!"

Anjali's hesitation had a reason to it. Of late, Sunil had started getting very worked up with Aakash's presence in almost everything they did.

"I know we owe him a huge lot in life," he stormed one day. "But isn't he becoming so omnipresent in our daily lives?"

Anjali just kept quiet. Somehow she had started feeling guilty about it of late. And her guilt was compounded by the fact that Tanvi had hardly taken to Sunil. The little child never hid her glee in being with Aakash Uncle!

The combined enthusiasm of Peter Jenkings and Anjali Sharma resulted in the rapid growth of the JGI (India) laboratory.

What was initially envisaged as being a small laboratory had now grown into a state-of-the-art genetic laboratory. The research work going on there was very comparable with that going on in laboratories around the world.

"There are of course, many areas of our research which must be kept under wraps, until we have some degree of success," Peter told the group of scientists who were now working in the laboratory. Peter had made four trips to Shillong in the last three years and was instrumental in getting the equipment shipped in to Shillong, setting up the labs, and in giving a direction to the research.

Anjali's role as the Director of the lab was that of a researcher, as well as of an administrator.

There were four British scientists in her group. They had obtained work permits from the Government of India, and were working on various aspects of therapeutic cloning. Peter would especially spend a lot of time with them, briefing them on what was expected out of them in the research.

At times Anjali got the feeling that in spite of being the Director of the laboratory, she wasn't aware of everything which was going on at the lab. Was she being deliberately left out from some of the research areas?

But then she would shrug it off, dismissing it as being a figment of her imagination, and probably there since her experience in the field of genetics was limited.

Aakash had, once again, engrossed himself in his clinic and in the little children of the Khasi villages in and around Shillong. His way of working was very different from that of other doctors. His clinic was just a small part of his life. He was more of a 'roaming' doctor. He would go into villages and sit with the elders, drinking the local rice-beer with them, learning of their problems, and lending a helping hand where possible.

He would sit with the little kids of the villages, sometimes teaching them, sometimes playing with them – seeking out their problems, and reaching out to them with a healing touch.

"*Khublei Shibun* – God bless and thank you," had become something he would hear so often, that it had become commonplace to him.

Most Khasis are now Christians. But very often, Aakash would sit with the little children and tell them stories of *U Blei Nongthaw* – the Supreme Being, The Creator, who the Khasis believed in earlier. He told them stories of the several deities of water and of the mountains who worked under *U Blei Nongthaw*.

And the children and the parents would take him to be one of their own - *Babha Kanthai* - a good doctor !

On Sundays, he would drive his Dinky into one of the villages, pack six or seven kids into her and then take them for a ride. The finale would always be a drive up to Laitkor Peak, where they would play for a little while, looking down at the scenic beauty of the city. Then they would race down the hill in Dinky, with the children yelling and screaming as if they were in a roller coaster ride.

The first time that Aakash felt intense pangs of jealousy was when they had all gone for a picnic to Cherrapunjee. It was Independence Day. The markets were closed, and so was the laboratory. The Sharma family had planned a picnic to the place, about 60 kilometers from Shillong, which was still known for being the wettest place on earth. In fact, it also holds a Guinness Book record for the maximum rainfall in a year – this was in the year 1860-61.

"Let me ask Aakash and his Dad to join us," said Anjali as she picked up the phone.

"Yippee!" yelled Tanvi.

On the other hand, Sunil hesitated. "Do you have to?" he asked. "Why can't just all of us go?"

"He knows the place well, Sunil" said Anjali.

"Yes, yes," said Karan. The kids seemed to have the veto in the house.

Mr. Anand had some other work to attend to, but Aakash readily joined them. In a way it was good for the Sharmas, since Aakash actually knew all the exciting places in and around Cherrapunjee.

Tanvi and Karan insisted on riding with him in Dinky. Hesitatingly, Aakash asked Anjali too. "Coming in Dinky?"

Anjali glanced at Sunil. "No," she said. "I think I'll go with Sunil and the rest."

They stopped at the Noh Kalikai falls on the way – just a few kilometers west of Cherrapunjee. They just stood there for a long time, taking in the breathtaking beauty of the place, watching the water emerge from a steep mountain bed, and then hurl down into a deep gorge.

It was all so romantic that Sunil reached out to hold Anjali's hand, and instinctively Aakash moved back, as if to get out of the way.

When they had had their fill of the scene, Aakash took over the role of the guide again. "Let me take you to see something you won't get to see elsewhere," he told them.

He took them to a village close to Cherrapunjee, called Nongriat.

"The War-Khasis had noticed the qualities of a certain species of the Indian rubber tree," Aakash told them. "They flourish alongside the many streams in Meghalaya. These trees have many secondary roots growing from their trunks. The War-Khasis would put hollowed out betel nut tree trunks across the rivers and then pass the roots through these trunks. The roots would grow through the trunks and reach the opposite bed of the river. With many of these, a bridge would form.

"See, look at that one," pointed out Aakash, as they walked through the village.

"Oh, wow – that's two – one on top of the other!" yelled Anjali excitedly as she pointed to what the locals call 'the Double-Decker Root Bridge'.

They started to cross on the lower bridge, and Aakash held out his hand to Anjali. But Sunil was right there, and he helped her across.

That was for the first time, that Aakash felt a pang of jealousy. Inwardly, he just shrugged and then turned round to Tanvi, who was waiting expectantly, for Aakash Uncle to carry her across.

But then it started happening very frequently. Small things would make Aakash brood. He was to collect a blood report of Tanvi's one day – and when he saw the name marked as Tanvi, with a Sharma as a surname, that spoilt his day. If he ever saw Anjali laughing and joking with Sunil, that spoilt his day. At times, even the mention of Sunil's name in their conversations would spoil his day!

Aakash tried to reason with himself. "She's married to Sunil," he would tell himself. "Obviously she has to pay more attention there."

The next minute, he would dispute his own argument. "But she is the one who kept telling me that our love is more important," he would think. "Then why is she changing?"

"You've changed, Aakash," Anjali said to him one day. "There's something on your mind, and you're not telling me!"

"No, Anjali, nothing at all," lied Aakash.

"And of late, you've stopped calling me Anju," she complained.

"No Anjali, I haven't," said Aakash.

"That's not how it used to be, Aakash," Anjali continued. "I thought friends were meant to share; and share everything!"

Aakash had a very faraway look as he said, "I didn't show you a poem that I wrote many years ago."

"You keep writing so many," said Anjali. "I'm suggesting this again - why don't you ever publish them? They'd make a great collection!"

"Would you ever publish your private thoughts?" he retorted.

Anjali kept quiet.

"Here, read this," said Aakash. He passed a handwritten notebook to her.

Anjali turned it over, to glance at the cover. Handwritten on the cover were the words of a famous old Bee Gees song – "*Its Only Words — And Words are All I Have, To Take Your Heart Away—*"

Anjali felt a lump in her throat as she realized what it was.

She flipped the pages, glancing through the book. There were at least a hundred poems written in the collection. She didn't have to read them to know that they were all about her.

Silently she read the poem that Aakash had pointed to. It ended poignantly with the lines:

. . . . .

. . . . .

Now that you have become
So very important to me,
All I want,
Is You !

She put the book down, and both of them sat quietly, just collecting their thoughts.

"You know very well that it's not possible - in this life, at least!" said Anjali finally.

"Why not?" asked Aakash. "There was a time when you said that our love was the most important to you."

"Yes, but Aakash, think back. You are the one who told me that marriage, as an institution, is so important. In the last four years, I've convinced myself that I must live with what I have. I know I've compromised. I know I could be much happier with another choice, but now I also know that in this life, I just have to live with it.

There was a small celebration at the laboratory when one of the teams working with Dr. Paul Boyle, was successful in cloning human embryos. This was done so that the stem cells could be harvested from the Blastoplast, and then, in future, be used for treating diseases.

Peter had a discussion with Anjali, and they decided that it would be best not to have too much of fanfare in Shillong, and make the announcement from the main lab in Manchester, so that too much media attention is not drawn towards the Shillong laboratory.

But immediately after this success, Anjali started having a lot of doubts in her mind about the ethical correctness of what they were doing. The thoughts were actually triggered when Aakash was sitting with her in the laboratory, discussing the progress of some of the projects. She was showing him around the labs, and had taken him to the sample room.

"Where do you get the eggs for the experiments which you all are doing?" asked Aakash.

"We've now got a group of ten women donors," said Anjali, introducing Aakash to Rishmesh Dawang. "Rishmesh here, has been of great help in getting us volunteers. And then we have another set of five male volunteers whose DNA is being used."

Rishmesh shook hands with Aakash.

"Here's your sixth volunteer," Anjali said, laughing and pointing to Aakash.

"But more seriously, show me how the sample is taken," said Aakash.

They went into the lab, where Rishmesh showed him the procedure, and in the process, took a sample from Aakash.

"What shall I do with this, ma'am?" he asked as they were leaving.

"Oh, just discard it," said Anjali. But in a moment, she turned back and said, "on the other hand, save it – you never know, we might have to grow another brain for him!"

She ducked, to avoid the punch which she expected from Aakash, but it never came.

When they came back into her office, they were still discussing the procedure of stem cell extraction, when Aakash brought up the issue of ethics.

"When you extract stem cells, aren't you destroying the embryo?" he asked.

"Yes, every time," answered Anjali. "That's after the egg has divided for about five days."

"But it's a human embryo, all the same," said Aakash. "You are actually causing the embryo to die!"

"Look at it the other way, Aakash. One day, these stem cells would be used to serve as replacement cells. We would be able to treat a variety of diseases, including cancer!"

Though she was arguing convincingly, Anjali did realize that she was talking Peter's language.

"I don't know," said Aakash, with a lot of doubts running through his mind. "Who gave you the right to play God?"

22

It was almost a year later, when Peter Jenkings came across to Shillong to spend two weeks at the laboratory. This time, he was accompanied by Lord Mehra. It was obvious that both of them were very pleased with the work going on in the lab and the tremendous progress made in the last five years. Twelve peer reviewed research papers had been published by the researchers working there. But whilst the affiliation of the researchers was indicated as JGI, Manchester, they all knew that the work was being done at Shillong.

During the trip, he got the researchers all together for a brainstorming session.

"You know we've made some terrific advancements in Somatic Cell Nuclear Transfer," he said.

He was referring to the procedure which, in the not-so-advanced form, was used in the cloning of Dolly the sheep at the Roslin Institute in 1996.

Anjali knew that they had made significant advancements in the procedures and processes at their lab. They would take an egg from one of the volunteer female donors, and remove its nucleus, thus creating an enucleated egg. Then a cell from a male volunteer, containing the DNA needed, would be fused with the enucleated egg using an electric shock. The embryo would thus be created.

"You know that in cases of some animal cloning, there have been failures," Peter continued. "But with our work here, we are more than confident that we have overcome the reasons for those."

Peter glanced towards Lord Mehra, and then he continued. "What we are suggesting is that we leverage on our successful experiments in Somatic Cell Nuclear Transfer, and that we move rapidly towards reproductive cloning."

Across the table, there was a fusion of shock and excitement. Anjali found herself gaping with her mouth open. She shut it in a hurry.

"Gosh, so all these years, this is what Peter has been aiming towards!" she thought, rather aghast at the idea of human cloning being done at the laboratory.

Later on, when they were alone, Anjali expressed her reservations to Peter. "You know experiments on human cloning are banned in the UK," she said.

"But not here, as yet, Anjali," said Peter. "Don't react impulsively. Look at the broader picture. Look at the tremendous advances medical science would make if mankind can successfully clone itself!"

"There have been very odd failures while cloning animals," Anjali argued. "Dolly had to be euthanized – we can't do that with humans!"

"That was years ago," Peter answered. "You know that in this lab itself we've been so successful in methylation of DNA, and that we can correctly alter the donated DNA to the state of an early embryo. Where is the risk then?"

"I know, Peter," said Anjali. "I am not so worried about the technical issues in human cloning. I know we can do it successfully. But it would be totally unethical. We can't just take nature into our own hands!"

"Even if it would help mankind?" asked Peter.

"I would say, even if would help mankind," Anjali answered without hesitation.

They carried on arguing and discussing for a long time. Anjali would later realize that this was for the first time in the six years that she had known Peter, that she was standing her ground. This was for the first time that her conviction was overriding her awe of Peter Jenkings!

"I am not going to rush you," said Peter eventually. "Give it time; give it a thought. We'll move ahead only when you are convinced, and when the entire group here is convinced."

"I never will be, Peter," said Anjali firmly. "I'm pretty sure experimenting with human cloning is unethical – and I for one, have no intentions of playing God …!"

Aakash passed the folder on to Anjali.

"What's this?" she asked.

"Have a look," said Aakash. "And then tell me whether you like it."

Anjali looked through the pamphlets of the two bedroom, luxurious apartments being built by Hiranandani in Mumbai.

"They are lovely," said Anjali, a bit puzzled. "Beautiful, in fact. But …?"

"I've booked one for us," Aakash announced.

"Us …?" she asked.

"Yes, you and me," Aakash answered. "For when you decide to leave everything and come and live with me."

"You're nuts, Aakash!" was all that she could say.

"Possibly, but I'm serious," said Aakash.

"And what about Uncle?" asked Anjali. "You'll leave him alone?"

"He wouldn't mind," said Aakash. "I'm sure of that."

Anjali had a frown on her face, with her mind confused, but clear at the same time.

"You've changed so much, Aakash," said Anjali. "You're straying so much from what you used to advise me earlier!"

"Love's done that to me," said Aakash in a matter of fact way.

"It's not possible now, Aakash," said Anjali finally.

"But, why ...?" asked Aakash. "Tell me very sincerely, are you in love with your husband?"

Anjali hesitated. "I guess I am," she said. "In a very basic sort of way."

"But you are much more in love with me?"

Anjali didn't answer.

"Your silence says it all, Anjali," said Aakash, almost yelling now.

"No, it doesn't, Aakash," she answered equally loudly. "You don't understand me at all now."

Her eyes were moist, and Aakash thought she would cry. She wiped her eyes with her *chunni* and continued.

"But I think it's time you move out of this world of imagination now and understand reality! I know I could be much, much more happy with you, than with Sunil. But over the years, you yourself have convinced me that even if the marriage is not so important, the institution of marriage has a meaning.

Aakash's mind was going blank now.

"And finally," said Anjali, "I just can't leave the kids. They both are happy – even Tanvi takes Sunil to be her father. I just can't shatter their lives!"

Not knowing what else to say, Anjali got up and walked away, leaving Aakash absolutely shattered.

23

Nobody even realized when Aakash slipped into depression. From childhood, he had developed the habit of living with what he called 'shutters down' – hiding his true feelings, not letting anyone know when he was sad.

It carried on for a bit more than three months. Even Anjali didn't realize. Possibly the only one who had a faint notion was Aakash's father, who had called him one day to have a 'heart-to-heart' chat.

"Are you in love, son?" he asked.

"Oh, that's it, Dad," Aakash slapped his thigh as he answered. "I was wondering what it was!"

"I'm serious Aakash," he said sternly. "And so should you be."

"Okay, Okay," said Aakash. "Shoot…"

"I've noticed many times, but I've always hesitated to ask," said Mr. Anand. "Is there something between you and Anjali?"

Aakash took a deep breath, but said nothing.

"Don't, my son!" said Mr. Anand. "Anjali is a nice girl, she's a great girl. But we are in a society where falling in love with a married woman is not at all understood. It might be intriguing – but it will get you nowhere."

"I know, Dad," Aakash looked down as he answered. "But it just happened."

"Even the married woman in India, son …" his father said, "even she would take small jumps with you, and you would find it thrilling. But when it comes to taking the big leap, her morals will always win. Ultimately, you will only hurt yourself.

Being a doctor himself, Aakash knew he should take medication for his depression, but he didn't. It just carried on building up.

It was a Sunday. As was his ritual, Aakash picked up Dinky and drove it up to a village close to Laitkor Peak. Before leaving, he had breakfast with his dad, and spent almost a half hour with him, nitpicking on the painting which he was working on. On his way out, he picked up the telephone and dialed Anjali's number. But on the second ring, he changed his mind, and disconnected it.

The kids at the village were waiting for him. The six 'chosen' ones were dressed in colourful clothes, waiting for their outing with their Doctor Uncle.

They drove up to the Peak and found a spot where they played with the Frisbee which Aakash had carried along. When they were tired, they sat down on the stone benches as Aakash opened packets of wafers and bottles of Coke for them.

And then it was time for the ride down the hairpin bends from the

Peak down. The kids piled into Dinky, and Aakash drove up to the start of the twisting road. But then he stopped there.

"You all get off and watch from here," he told the children in Khasi. "Uncle will show you some tricks."

He revved up. The children yelled and screamed as usual. The jeep picked up speed and the children watched wide eyed, with their mouths open as it went over the big hump at the edge of the road. It seemed as if it hung in the air for a while and then pitched down and went over the cliff.

The little urchins watched, fascinated, as it tumbled down the hill. They clapped furiously until they saw bigger people come rushing up to the edge of the cliff. They saw the jeep exploding in a ball of fire as it continued going down. And then they stopped clapping as they realised that something was wrong - something was terribly, terribly wrong.

Epilogue

The lone, adventurous squirrel finally built up guts to scamper up to where Anjali was sitting on a tree stump in the backyard of her house. It stood on its hind legs and looked at Anjali, cocking its head to one side as if to say, "No tid-bits today?"

After Tanvi had left to go in to have her lunch, Anjali had continued sitting there, reminiscing about the past, living the last two hours or so with Aakash's memories. She was still staring at the trees when the squirrel climbed onto the close by stump of another tree on which Anjali had put a book and a file. As the squirrel jumped on top, the book tipped over and fell, startling both, itself and Anjali. The squirrel ran away into the woods and Anjali finally got up after her train of thought was broken.

She picked up the file from the stump and then bent down to pick up the book, deciding now to go back into the house. As it was, it had become very chilly. When she picked up the book, she saw the loose sheet of paper which had fallen out. Opening it, she realized that it was the poem which she had written. On numerous occasions, Aakash had tried to convince her to write some poetry, but she had always resisted.

"Don't be silly, Aakash," she had said. "Imagine me writing poetry! It'll probably be as good as your drawings!"

"No, Anju," he had said. "We all have emotions. And most of us want to express them, or share them with someone who cares. So we talk – or maybe, write a diary. Well, poetry is just another form of letting out your innermost feelings."

Just four days back, when Aakash was upset with her, she had withdrawn into her office in the laboratory and had penned down a poem – her first. She meant to tear it up, but when she went over it again, she changed her mind.

"Not bad," she thought. "Not bad at all for a beginning. I must show it to Aakash."

She had folded it and kept it in the book, meaning to read it out to Aakash. Somehow in the last four days, she never got a chance.

Now it was too late.

Anjali went back to the stump and sat on it once again. She opened the sheet of paper and read out to herself:

My heart knows not what it wants.

But it needs you with every beat it takes.

My mind knows not what it wants.

But it always conjures pictures of you.

On moments,

I have wanted to rush into your arms.

On moments,

I have wanted to rest my head

on your shoulders and cry.

But destiny had other intentions.
It had a path drawn out for this life!
And as the world moves on,
nobody , but you ,
notices my loneliness in the crowd.
Nobody , but you ,
sees the moistness in my eyes.
Nobody , but you ,
fills the voids in my path.
So often have I hurt you.
But that is because words
have never been able to traverse
the distance from my heart to my mouth.

Actions have never been able to traverse
the distance from my mind to my arms.
Twenty four small inches
have felt like light years to me.
So whenever you get angry at me
you must understand ,
that you are only angry
at my words and my actions.
And not at my heart or my mind
For those
Will live on forever for you!

As she read the last two lines, she realized that she had a catch in her voice. She smiled wryly to herself and then tore up the paper into small pieces. She kept folding the paper and tearing it into smaller pieces until finally she couldn't tear them any smaller. Then she threw them into the wind. The pieces scattered – some into the air, some onto the ground. But all of them were blown away from her. She felt herself heaving and she couldn't stop the tears that welled up in her eyes. "How am I going to live the rest of my life without him?" she thought.

"Was it just like a dream?" Anjali wondered. "A dream which has passed; and left me now to live a different life. Or was that my life which has passed and left me now to live in a zombie-like existence?"

"Maybe Sunil's philosophy- or is it lack of philosophy- was the best," she thought. "Don't be too close to anyone. That way you don't get hurt."

"Or maybe Aakash was right all along. Maybe I should have had the guts to have gone away with him. Maybe that would have kept both of us happy for the rest of our lives."

She had questions, but she had no answers.

"It was so easy consoling relatives of patients at hospitals," she thought. "… telling them that everything that God did was for the best."

Now she wondered how she could have talked like that. What God…, which God? Isn't God only for fairy tales or for Bollywood movies, which always have happy endings?

She had encountered death so many times in hospitals. But that had been so different. It had been like watching a cricket match on a television set sitting in the cozy comforts of a living room. The players were far away – very far away; figures who were only names to her. Their getting bowled or run out only extracted groans or disappointment for a few moments. But here she was – batting for life and suddenly her middle stump had been uprooted. She had no clue as to what she should do next. She wasn't even aware that she had to leave the crease and walk out of the playing field!

"In our next life, we'll be together," she had once told Aakash.

And Aakash had joked about it. "Yes, positively," he had said. "When I die, I'll carry a bottle of Scotch with me to bribe God with, so that when he does the allotments, he doesn't allot you to another joker!"

Aakash had always lived life for the present. He seemed to be in a hurry to do things straight away – as if there was no tomorrow. Today Anjali realized what Aakash meant by 'it's now or never'. Death carries a ring of finality, that comes along with it. *Tat Sat* – or that's it. Amen. Over and out – as a signaler might say. But none of us want to accept that. We want life to carry on. We want our lives and the lives of our loved ones to carry on endlessly. But we also know that death creeps on us suddenly and numbs us. So we create and live in the hope that life carries on after death.

Even in this skepticism, Anjali felt herself taking a deep breath and involuntarily looking up at the sky.

"So what if you won't be in front of me, Aakash," she said half aloud. "You taught me never to give up. You were a coward – you gave up. But I won't. You just watch what I do next!"

She got up suddenly. It was as if she was filled with a maniacal determination. There were no tears in her eyes as she strode back into the house. She had, in a flash, made up her mind. "Now you watch, Aakash," she said half to herself. "Now you watch – I'm going to play God!"

"Are you going somewhere, Mama?" asked Tanvi, looking up from the Enid Blyton which she was reading.

Tanvi squirmed with pleasure as Anjali picked her up and hugged her.

"Yes, sweetheart," said Anjali. "I'm going to the laboratory. Where's Papa?"

"He's in the bedroom, playing video games."

"Okay, I'm rushing off," said Anjali. "You tell him I'll be back in a couple of hours."

In the laboratory, she walked straight into the sample storage room. A whole lot of samples and specimens were neatly labeled and stored. Most of them had an immediate purpose in the ongoing research. Some of them were just marked and stored for possible future use.

She looked around for one particular specimen. After ten minutes of rummaging, she gave up. She couldn't find what she was looking for.

"What if it's been misplaced?" she asked herself. "But how can that be – where would a specimen go?"

She was getting worried now. Very quickly, she opened her office. She put on the computer and waited impatiently for it to boot up. When it did, it asked her for a password. Anjali keyed in 'hii'- which looked innocuously like an enthusiastic greeting to the machine, but actually was an acronym of the last letters of the names of the three people who, till a couple of days ago, made up her virtual family – Aakash, Tanvi, Anjali. As the customized desktop came on, she double clicked on the icon marked 'specimens'. A database in EXCEL opened. She queried it but found no matching results. She queried it again and again in different forms. Each time the results were the same. Obviously the data of that specimen had been deleted. Or probably the specimen had been erroneously used in some other experiment.

For a while, she slumped back in her chair, feeling totally deflated. So God had won. He wasn't going to let her play His role.

With only a bit of hesitation, she moved the mouse pointer to the 'start' menu and then clicked on 'shut down'. The computer gave her one more chance to reconsider – and she felt like clicking on 'cancel' and going back to the search once again. But she knew it was futile. As the screen flickered and went off, she felt a wave of loneliness going through her again.

She was sitting quietly, leaning back on her chair, with her mind fairly blank, when she heard some noise in the lab. When she came out, she found that Rishmesh Dawang, the research assistant working with her, had come in and was setting up some equipment.

"Hi," said Anjali, quite surprised to see him. "What're you doing here so late?"

"Evening ma'am," Rishmesh smiled at her. "Something struck me at home, and I thought I'd come into the lab and check it out."

Anjali started to go out, when Rishmesh came up to her. "Ma'am, I'm so sorry to hear about Doctor Anand," he said softly. "It must have been such a shock to you."

"Yes, Rishmesh," said Anjali. "It was. In fact I came in here looking for the specimen of his which we had taken a few months back. Do you remember – you were there, I think."

"Of course – I remember," said Rishmesh.

"It's not there on the computer," Anjali sounded defeated. "I've spent the last ten minutes looking for it."

"It won't be ma'am," said Rishmesh. "You said to just keep it in the specimen room and not to enter it in the data because it was taken with no purpose at all."

"But where is the specimen?"

"I know where it is," Rishmesh said, heading off into the specimen room. He came out just a few moments later holding a bottle in his hand.

Excited, Anjali took the bottle in her hand and looked at the label –

which said, rather plainly – 'Aakash Anand, Male, 46 yrs, specimen date: 13 Jul 2004'.

She told Rishmesh to keep it separately, as she rushed back to her office and put on the computer once again. She logged on to the internet and after she opened her e-mail account, she sat back to type:

Dear Dr Jenkings,

With reference to the numerous conversations, discussions, arguments and mail exchanges which we have had on the subject – I've once again given a lot of thought to it. I have now changed my mind and am ready to go ahead with the project.

I have two pre-conditions before we go on. First, it is I who will decide which specimen is to be used for the project. Secondly, it is I who will get custody of what we produce.

I already have a volunteer to be a surrogate mother. I already have the specimen. And I am ready to begin work right away. I will be speaking to the team, and I am sure we will all be in agreement. As desired, we will keep the whole project under wraps till we succeed.

In India we say "Shree Ganesh" when we start anything new – and I am saying that right now as I begin. Fifteen days from now we should be able to do the in vitro fertilization.

And nine and a half months from now, we would be able to present to the world, the first cloned human being!

Regards,

Anjali.